WOMEN AND ANGELS

The Author's Workshop

THE JEWISH PUBLICATION SOCIETY OF AMERICA
PHILADELPHIA · NEW YORK · JERUSALEM
5745 · 1985

HAROLD BRODKEY

WOMEN AND ANGELS

Copyright © 1985 by Harold Brodkey
First edition
Manufactured in the United States of America

Library of Congress Cataloging in Publication Data

Brodkey, Harold.
  Women and angels.
  (The Author's workshop)
  Contents: Ceil — Lila — Angel.
  I. Title.   II. Series.
PS3552.R6224W6   1984   813'.54   84–25000
ISBN 0–8276–0250–2

Designed by ADRIANNE ONDERDONK DUDDEN

The Author's Workshop is a series of limited first editions by significant American writers who are choosing to address a Jewish audience—some for the first time. Each volume represents a unique publishing story: Concentrating on imaginative writing, it includes works in progress as well as recent works that have never been printed until now or have not previously appeared in book form. Each volume begins with an original autobiographical introduction. The book as a whole will not again be available to the public. These limited editions are conceived primarily for the members of the Jewish Publication Society, who have been supporting innovative Jewish publishing in America for almost one hundred years.

Probably best known for its Bible translations, JPS has taken the initiative in developing all aspects of Jewish culture—religion, art, poetry, literature in translation, history, legend, pioneering scholarship and classics of Jewish thought, both modern and time-honored. Continuing its original mandate to shape the growth of Jewish culture in its American form, JPS is now aware of a new Jewish audience, sophisticated enough to confront its history and resources in a creative way. *The Author's Workshop* is the first of several series which are planned to stimulate the definition and growth of Jewish culture in America by focusing on its imaginative writers. As recently as twenty years ago, it was rare that someone not brought up as a Jew would address a secular Jewish audience, such as is now in resurgence in America as well as in Israel.

Just as each generation of artists in a free society has to decide for itself what painting or poetry should be, each generation of Jewish artists defines its Jewishness. What counts in both art and Judaism is not only spectacular beginnings but also the power of renewal. Today, what is missing is not the authors but the context in which Jewish books can receive the care and devotion they deserve. JPS, in establishing these new series of books to nurture a Jewish context, is helping to create a sense of community to inspire authors as well as readers. Jewish memory has been rejuvenated with JPS translations; in the same tradition, *The Author's Workshop* is a pioneering presentation of contemporary Jewish authors.

Women and Angels by Harold Brodkey represents the first book publication of significant portions from the author's long-anticipated major novel, which is nearing completion.

CONTENTS

 WOMEN AND ANGELS

AUTHOR'S INTRODUCTION

To die as a Jew, among Jews, because I was a Jew, that defined the matter for me when I was a child. This was in the Midwest in the 1930s. Precocious and somewhat earnest, I was an informal oracle, a semi-rebbe for the superstitious around me, and that was the formulation I arrived at. The Nazis were widely admired, and the Jews had no allies that I knew of. At one time, there had been something thought of as Jewish power, an amalgam of scholars, scientists, artists, journalists, and bankers, taken all in all to represent a force in the destiny of Europe and, therefore, of the world; the Nazis had shown that force to be helpless—Nazism was perceived as an effective tool for controlling any such reality of Jewish influence on events. It seemed to me the destruction of the Jews would reach Missouri, where I lived.

That was one part of what I was. Another part had to do with a complex situation that went like this: I had been adopted when I was two, when my real mother died. My real family tried to get me back when I was five; they wanted me to be a rebbe for real. They spoke of the money and power and respect accorded a rebbe. I thought about it.

And I talked to people and I read the Bible (in English) and one or two books on Talmud. My childhood decision was that observance was not the heart or soul of Judaism; a balance point, a source of warmth but of uncertain merit outside the sense of worth and purpose given a family or a group of families. I lived in a fairly prosperous suburb, and felt that sacredness, while it existed in full measure in this country, seemed singularly unable to inspire Protestant or Catholic or Jewish observance here: The uninspired architecture of the churches and the uninspired liturgies seemed to me to be a sign. I placed myself in a category, foolishly, that of being an American in an uncertain way; so that as the war wore on and spread, it seemed to me I would have to die as an American among Americans as well.

Those families in which observance is the primary element of their Judaism (or rather, those groups of families, since such Judaism does not permit singularity of devotion or individual piety) do not in numbers or in their sense of sacredness, in my belief, supply a definition for me, an American and a Jew, of what it is to be Jewish. When I consider Jewish history, it seems they never have been the sole creative element—in the long history of ancient Israel, in the sum of the diasporas, or in modern Israel—and that to think they have been is sentimental.

Important, yes, and of scholarly merit, although not so much in this country as elsewhere, and attractive to me—I am drawn to observance, to strict observances, and to the rage of nagging and denouncing those less strict—but it seems to me that those who do that, including me, are defensive and do not give credit to those who do more truly support Israel and those others who have, in my view, truer ideas about Judaism itself.

To me, those whose sense of sacredness is satisfied by being observant in the old way resist the evident—not the codified—will of The Unnamed, and they do it in a state of emotional comfort and angry self-righteousness. I believe that they believe that they avert God's wrath by their observance. I think that observance is a great help in ethical matters and as communal discipline but that it interferes with sacredness.

I think Jewish sacredness is more intelligent than that available in Christianity—or in Jewish orthodoxy—and is the highest level of transcendence yet reached; and its prophets are many, and so are its demons and its heretics.

I think I have said perhaps too much on this subject already—but I will add that nothing in this short note is said for effect: This is what I think is the truth in these matters.

The pieces of fiction in this volume are concerned with my belief, in the sense of literal secular experiences, and in the sense of my experience of sacredness. The first two pieces have previously appeared in *The New Yorker*, "Lila" in slightly different form under another title. "Angel" has not previously appeared in print. Although they are parts of a larger work nearing completion, this is my first collection of pieces from it in a book.

CEIL

I have to imagine Ceil—I did not know her; I did not know my mother. I cannot imagine Ceil. She is the initial word. Everything in me having to do with knowing refers to her. The heart of the structures of my speech is my mother. It is not with my mother but with Ceil in her own life that my speech begins. My mother as an infant, and then a child, and then a girl, a hoyden maybe, seven years old, ten and coldly angular, and then a girl of twelve, then a girl of nineteen, tall, thin-bodied, long-legged in a fashion inconceivable to me. What I am is her twisted and bereaved and altered and ignorant heir. She died when I was two. I died as well, but I came to life again in another family, and no one was like her, everything was different. I was told I was not like her. I see that she is not human in the ways I am: She is more wise, more pathetic—whichever—in some way larger than my life, which, after all, she contained for a while. I was her dream, her punishment. She dreams me but she bears me, too. Her dream is real. It is a clouded and difficult legend.

I tend to feel an almost theatrical fright when I am near a subject that hints of her. I've felt this way since I was six and learned that my real mother had died and that I did not know her.

In the last year before the war that shaped her life, in 1913, she was nineteen; and she has a too stylishly formed, too stylized a body, too sexual, too strongly marked for me to be comfortable with the thought of her. Her body when she was that age I recognize; I invent it. I know her feet, her hands, her hair—as a girl: They are unlike mine. She has longish brown hair, very fine-drawn, so that, although it is curly, its own weight straightens it except at the ends. Fine hair, which sets an uneasy and trembling too-thin silkiness, a perilously sexual lack of weight around her face, which bobs nakedly forward from what might have framed or hidden her vitality; beneath the too-fine hair is one of those girlishly powerful faces atop a tall body, a face large-lipped, eyes set very wide; a face bold with an animal and temperamental and intellectual electricity. She is both regal and peasantlike, gypsyish—or like a red Indian—a noticeable presence, physically exhilarated and willful. She is muscular. She is direct in glance. She has a long neck and a high rear end and longish feet and short-fingered hands with oddly unimpressive nails—her hands are not competent; they are cut off a little from life because her mind is active and her hands consequently stumble, but her energy and a somewhat hot and comic and even farcical grace of attention she has make up for that, and she is considered by others and by herself to be very good at manual things anyway.

And she is literate—she is bookish and given to quoting and argument—and she is active physically, and she is given to bad temper rather than to depression. In comparative poverty, in an era of grave terrors, she has lived in enough danger that she has become courteous and ironic, and has been ever since she was a small child, but the courtesy and the irony lie atop a powerful other self. As a personality, she was a striking image for others from the beginning—she was what would be called by some people A Great Favorite: much pawed is what that comes down to. This is among Jews and Russians. Things were asked of her often by her mother and her father and by others: errands and talk and company, physical company. She was noticeable and had that quality of mind which made people take her as *special*, as being destined and far-seeing, more *reasonable* than others. She was (in a sense) the trademark or logo of the community, of the family—sought after, liked, used, I would imagine, but she was patient with that because she was praised, and so admiringly looked at as well. People close their minds off and charge and butt at their favorites—or tease and torment them: A Peasant Beauty.

Here are some sentences from Chekhov: *The village was never free of fever, and there was boggy mud there even in the summer, especially under the fences over which hung old willow-trees that gave deep shade. Here there was always a smell from the factory refuse and the acetic acid which was used in the finishing of cotton print. . . . The tanyard often made the little river stink . . .* [Bribes to the chief of police and the district doctor kept the factory open.] *In the whole village there were only two decent houses made of brick with tin roofs.*

And: *The sonorous, joyful clang of the church bells hung over the town unceasingly, setting the spring air aquiver.*

And: *The charming street in spring, on each side of it was a*

*row of poplars. . . . And acacias, tall bushes of lilacs, wild
cherries and apple-trees hung over the fence and the palings.*

Barefoot, in Russia near a small ravine, she moves, much
too showily present, not discreet, not slipping and sliding
along in the Oriental fashion, not devious or subterranean
or flirtatious or in any masquerade, but obvious and present, forthright in a local manner, a common enough manner
in that part of the world where women ran farms and inns
and stores and had that slightly masculinized swagger or
march, that alive-in-the-world-of-men, alert, and rough-
ened air, that here-and-now way of presenting themselves.

Ceil, almost nervously, always overrated rebellion—and
discipline—loyalty to the absent *king*, complete law-abid-
ingness as rebellion, the claim of following the true law,
the truer one.

In Illinois, where money was comparatively plentiful,
she would despise money, which she liked; but despising it
was a further mode of bandit independence and religious,
soaring freedom. She would be confused by the utter se-
crecy of the actual politics of the county and the state, the
bribes and the use of force and the criminal nature of much
that goes on; she will not understand the sheer power of
the lie in creating a password-based social class of rule, of
stability: this Christian doubleness, perhaps largely English in style in Illinois, will strike her as contemptible.

(*She was always talking about being realistic; she wanted
everyone to be realistic about everything all the time; she lorded
it over everyone because she was so realistic.* The woman who
became my mother, Lila Silenowicz, told me this.)

She never lived in a city. Well, actually she did try to
live in St. Louis for a while, but the urban sophistications,

the interplay of things, of money and information and shibboleth—respectabilities and concealed coercions—upset her, and I believe she lost out in whatever she tried to do, in whatever she attempted in the way of dignity there.

And Max's proposal, my father's proposal, offered her a life in a small town, a really small town—thirty-five hundred people. Long after Ceil died, my mother by adoption said, "Ceil wanted a foothold. She wasn't really under anyone's protection. She could do what she wanted; no one could stop her. No one wanted her to listen to Max; he was no good, no good for a woman; but it didn't matter what anyone thought; she could do as she liked." Max's proposal involved her going to live in that small town, under an enormous canopy of sky like that pale canopy that overhangs plains anywhere, and it's true that her pride and victories took root again once she was in so small a place.

My mother's mind, and to some extent her language, tribal and local but influenced by St. Petersburg, and her conceit are somewhat like those of the poet Mandelstam, who was born not far from where she was born. He lived at the same time; similar dates cover his life, too, but it was a different life, of course, except that it, too, was stubborn and mad, and his death was as empty of reason as Ceil's.

Mandelstam went to St. Petersburg, and he went south a number of times, to the Crimea. He went to school in St. Petersburg, and he was considerably more *civilized* than Ceil was, early or late, and stiff-necked and romantic and unromantic, and as passionately self-willed and oddly placed in the world as she was: he was deathful and lifeful in similar ways. He has a line in a poem which I will say goes into English as (it is about the dome of Hagia Sophia, in Istanbul) *"It is swimming in the world."* It is swimming in the world at the end of a long gold chain let down from Heaven.

On a dusty road, here is Ceil, here is my mother, and she is like that in her mind.

Ceil thought of herself as a Jew first, then as a woman, and, when I knew her, she thought of herself as an American—she had no interest in being European.

Her father, it was known, could talk to God; he could influence God; God cared about him. On certain special (cathedral, or sanctified) occasions, Ceil's father could tug the gold chain let down from Heaven.

"Ceil didn't like him so much—she loved him; she was a good daughter, don't get me wrong—but everyone thought only about him, and it suffocated her. She had a bad streak; she thought she was as smart as anyone." (Lila. My mother by adoption.)

Ceil was an immensely passionate woman, who loved steadily and somewhat harshly in the nature of things; that is, that was the form her energy and attention outwardly took.

"She loved to work; she loved to keep things clean. She loved to have you on her arm. She loved to have her hair done. She didn't giggle none." (This is Old Ruthie talking. My grandmother by adoption.) "She had no foolishness; she liked to work."

"She was a cold woman, pardon me for saying it—very cold. But you couldn't tell with her. She liked that little town; she liked Max for a while. You never knew with her

—she sometimes seemed very hot, even sentimental, to me; I was colder in the long run. But she said she was alone; she said she had always been alone until you were born, and now she had someone and she was happy. It's too bad it didn't last." (Lila.)

"Ceil was big; she carried herself like a queen; she couldn't come into a room quietly, you know." (Lila.)

My grandfather was a ferocious Jewish charlatan. Unless he actually was a magician. Ceil believed in him. The family myth is that he was a wonder-working rebbe, who had a private army and a small group of industries that he ran and, because he was a religious genius, fifteen thousand loyal followers at his command—a man six feet six or seven or four or five, a man unashamed of his power in the world, his influence over men and over women, a man who could *scare a Cossack.*

But I don't believe it. It is not true. It is mostly untrue, I think. He was poor, and his congregation was poor.

Lila: "Ceil said she hardly knew her mother. There were fifteen, twenty, twenty-five children by the same woman. Ceil said she was a shadow. Ceil said she paid no attention to anyone but the father. Ceil was the youngest, the last one. It used to embarrass Ceil to tell this. Ceil said the father was too smart and too religious to like women. If you ask me, he didn't care about anything but himself; your grandmother got the benefit and the work. . . ."

And: *She was his shadow; she liked it like that; Ceil didn't like that, she didn't want to be like that, she told me she didn't want a man she had to feel obligated to at all.*

Ceil's mother spun and flamed and guttered out her life, my grandma, in hero worship (maybe).

Lila: "Your mother was raised by her older sister."

Lila: "Ceil never knew what kind of man Max was. What could she know? She was ignorant; she only knew what she knew, you know what I mean? She knew what she could know. I wish you understood me, Wiley."

The stories of women go unheard, I understood her to say, Lila.

"No one knows what happens to women. No one knows how bad it is, or how good it is, either. Women can't talk —we know too much."

Ceil's father, my grandfather, claimed literally to be the unnamable God's vicar on earth, his voice on earth—poor or not.

I mean, within four walls he was magnificent, not boastful but merely dutiful toward his powers: He was as powerful as Bach.

She, Ceil, was his pet. She is physically very striking, even exotic, not Jewish-exotic but Tatar-exotic—Byzantine, Saracen. And she has a mind of notable quality, a rankling form of forwardness that shows itself early, and she is educated more than a Jewish woman usually is in such communities, since her father considers her remarkable in her way and thinks that she might be a prophet and his true heir more than his thick-witted and numberless sons.

For a woman, surely, words are the prime element of force, of being able to enforce things on others, to coerce them. The prime *realistic* thing, in a certain sense, for women in this world, is words, words insofar as they contain law and announcements of principles, the semi-minor apocalypses of utopia, or at least of peace on earth. For Lila, too, it was criticism, judgment, social and psychological coercion. But for Ceil most words were God's, and were cabalistic: The right terms could summon happiness.

Lila: "She hated the Communists by the time they were through; she said they wouldn't give anyone any peace; she said they were mean and stupid, amen."

And: "She had wonderful skin, and she was a good sleeper: I think she had a good conscience; she was very strict. She wasn't shy with people. She wasn't scared; she could talk to anyone; she was like a queen. Your mother had a nice laugh, but she wouldn't laugh in front of men— she said it was like showing her drawers. I never saw anyone as sure of herself as she was—it could drive you crazy sometimes. I never saw her tired."

Life is unlivable, but we live it. No virgin would have married Max Stein. No good-hearted daughter of a strikingly holy man would have left such a presence.

He wants to marry her to a scholar, a rachitic and skinny scholar, devoted to *pilpulim* and to certain Chassidic songs, certain spells of rapture, certain kinds of cunning wit, and, above all, to him, the rebbe, the physical and sexual and worldly power who has been the holy body for the thinner bodies who are his flock. The skinny and lesser mystic he has chosen, and Ceil will preserve the line. In the past Ceil was intoxicated by such notions, but now it is too late.

Events have aged her. The war. A brother's disappearance. Perhaps something personal—a man, a woman. A book. A movie. A grief. Or greed: *She wanted a chance to live.* Ceil will choose sin and will be an outcast.

Tall, long-legged, the odd-eyed young woman resists, refuses the marriage. ("There was real trouble between her and her father. He forgave her and he put a curse on her both. He was ugly about her. But she was selfish. She wasn't afraid of him any more.")

Ceil wasn't ashamed of anything. That's one reason she married Max, so she wouldn't be ashamed of the people back in the old country—the court. *She did things, oddly, for her father and against him. She straightened out her life for his sake, in a way.*

Lila: "She went to the beauty parlor twice a week and she liked Garbo. She didn't speak English and she worked as a maid, I think. She wanted to have her own money, her own life, right away. She had offers, but she turned them all down. She always acted as if she knew what she was doing."

I start with Garbo; I think of scenes of Garbo *traveling*—that almost impossibly powerful presence on the screen, at once challenging and Nordically disciplined, costumed, unafraid.

And: "Your mother was always quick to dress herself up. You'd say about another woman she was putting on airs, but you wouldn't say it about her—it was just one of the things she liked and she made it seem religious almost, a duty. She was like a queen that way."

My father, Max, came from Odessa. My mother did not meet him there, but she sailed from Odessa on a grain ship, and she landed in New Orleans.

Lila: "No one met her, not one of her relatives—she only had one sister in this country—but I swear to God she wasn't frightened. The first thing she did was have her hair done. I won't say she was vain; it wasn't like vanity in her, it was something else. But she went out on the street afterward, and she saw what she had done to it was wrong. What money she had she was never afraid to spend on herself. Oh, you don't have any grip on what she was like. She could live on cabbage or on air; she could walk and not take a streetcar. She had a terrible amount of energy, you know. Anyway, she went to a better beauty parlor right away, the same day, the same hour, and had her hair done all over again, so no one would laugh at her. She was an immigrant, but she knew what was what from the beginning."

And: "After a while, she married Max and went to that little town. She did laugh a lot, always, but it was often cruel, very cruel—her jokes were mean. But sometimes she was just like a girl. She would never go shopping with me. I used to give her things—silk scarves, jewelry—but then she stopped taking things. I never knew what to make of her."

Giggling, she journeys by bus or train up the Mississippi Valley, Memphis, St. Louis, inland in Illinois.

Lila: "She used to let us all lie on her bed, and she would tell stories until we were faint with laughter. If you ask me, she wasn't prepared for her sister's not being high society. Her sister must have lied a lot when she wrote home—you know how it is—and Ceil made jokes about it."

17 · *Ceil*

And: "Ceil made money from the first, writing letters for people to the old country, and she worked in a restaurant, but that was dirty and hard, and then she took to working in people's houses because she was safer there from men, and after the first year she started speaking English better."

One story about Ceil's father, who was killed nearly ten years after Ceil died, was that the Russians (in another war) ordered him and his congregation to evacuate, to retreat to the east. He, for one reason or another—disloyalty to Stalin among his reasons—refused to accede to that order to migrate to Siberia. He was in his eighties. Eighteen shots—so the family myth goes—were fired at him by the Russians, but the Germans were near and the Russians fled, and he was healed or miraculously had not been hit or was so wounded it didn't matter to him if he lived or died, and he lived in an in-between state until the Germans came, and he confronted them, too, a living dead man in his anger, and the Germans shot him, in mid-curse, in front of the Ark. Some part of this is true, is verifiable.

Lila: "Ceil betook herself from her sister's, and she went to St. Louis, where some educated Jews lived and there was a good rabbi. Some people took her in, but she worked as a maid, and they used her—she didn't know how not to work; she was accustomed to doing everything for her father—and she thought the St. Louis rabbi was silly and knew nothing—she said he had no God—and she had offers, but they didn't interest her. But everybody liked her, we all liked her, and wondered what would happen to her, and she married Max. We warned her, but she was stubborn—she would never listen to anyone."

Here is Ceil in America, in Illinois—in a little town of thirty-five hundred—among American faces, cornfields, American consciences and violence; and her earlier memories never leave her, never lose their power among the sophistications of this traveler in her costumes, her days, her mornings and evenings. I think it was like that. Of course, I know none of this part as a fact.

She lived at the edge of the farm town, in a wooden house —it had five finished rooms in it. Across the road, the farm fields begin on the other side of a shallow ditch. Those fields stretch without a hill to the horizon. Never is the landscape as impressive as the skyscape here. From the rear of the house to the center of town is perhaps two and a half blocks. The houses are close together. Nowadays, there are trailers set up permanently on these streets where there were lawns once. It's not a rich town. To the east, between the town and the superhighway, which is seven miles away, two slag heaps rise in the middle of cornfields. In the course of a day, the shadows of the slag heaps make a clocklike round on the leaves of the corn around them.

In the summer, the laboring factory sky and the rows of corn in their long vegetable avenues form an obscene unity of heat. In winter, the sky is a cloud-jammed attic, noisy and hollow.

She was ashamed, you know—her accent, her size. She knew she was something and that people admired her, and still she hid herself away. She could see her way to a dime, her eyes would light up over seventy-five cents—I could never do that. She was good at arithmetic, she could do numbers in her head better than a man, and she could make people laugh, and no one thought she was a liar: You don't know what that means in a little town—everyone keeps track of who makes money, and if anyone makes money people think he's gouging everyone else. She had a good eye for just how good she could do on a deal and still go on in that town; she was honest, but she was a good liar, and she socked some money away so people wouldn't hold it against her; she was getting richer by the day, by leaps and bounds, and she wanted a child to make her life complete.

You were her success in the world, you were her success in America in a nutshell.

I was born in her bedroom, at home.

I *feel* her; I feel her moods.

Alongside the house and running at a diagonal to it is a single-track railroad. It is set on a causeway six feet high. I think I can remember the house begin to shake with an amazing faint steadiness until, as if in an arithmetical theater, the house begins to slide and shimmy in a quickening rhythm that is not human. It is as if pebbles in a shaking drum became four, then eight, then rocks, perhaps like

numbers made of brass in a tin cylinder, antic and chatter-
ing like birds, but more logically. In lunacy, the sound in-
creases mathematically, with a vigor that is nothing at all
like the beating of a pulse or the rhythms of rain. It is loud
and real and unpicturable. The clapboards and nails, glass
panes and furniture and wooden and tin objects in drawers
tap and whine and scratch with an unremitting increase in
noise so steadily there is nothing you can do to resist or
shut off these signals of approach. The noise becomes a
yawing thing, as if the wall had been torn off the house and
we were flip-flopping in chaos. The noise and echoes come
from all directions now. The almost unbearable bass of the
large interior timbers of the house has no discernible pattern but throbs in an aching shapelessness, isolated.

At night, the light on the locomotive comes sweeping
past the trembling window shades, and a blind glare pours
on us an unstable and intangible milk in the middle of the
noise. The rolling and rollicking thing that rides partway
in the sky among its battering waves of air does this to you.
Noise is all over you and then it dwindles; the shaking and
noise and light flow off, trickle down and away, and the
smell of the grass and of the night that was there before is
mixed with the smell of ozone, traces of burnt metal, a
stink of vanished sparks, bits of smoke from the engine if
the night is without wind.

The train withdraws and moves over the fields, over the
corn. The house ticks and thumps, tings and subsides. The
train moves southwest, toward St. Louis.

The wooden-odored shade of a porch, the slightly acid smell of the house: soap and wood—a country smell.

My mother's torso in a flowered print dress.

A summer, an autumn, a winter—those that I had with Ceil.

The house had very large windows that went down quite close to the floor. These windows had drawn shades that were an inhumanly dun-yellow color, a color like that of old lions in the zoo, or the color of corn tassels, of cottonwood leaves after they have lain on the ground for a while—that bleached and earthen clayey white-yellow.

My mother's happiness was not the concern of the world.

I half believe that my mother had a lover. I half remember going with her to see him; she took me with her on a train that ran by electricity among the flat farm fields. I stood on the seat and looked out the train window. My hand marks and nose marks and breath marks—I remember those and her hand wiping the marks away. I see wheeling rows of corn, occasional trees, windmills, farmhouses.

Maybe I am mistaken.

LILA: *She had more character than any woman I ever knew, but a lot of good it did her.*

Your mother knew she'd made a mistake marrying Max; she gave him money and she knew he would spend it and go off: She was no one's fool, but how she had the nerve to live in that little town alone I just don't know; everyone's watching; you can fall flat on your face.

Ceil's business did well in hard times and in good times. My brother said she was a genius at business—she had such a good head men were interested in doing business with her—men enjoyed talking to her, she was their size, and you could see she was religious, she was serious; it tickled people that someone so smart lived in such a little town and worked so hard and didn't speak English well and was getting ahead in the world anyway.

You won't understand this, but she wasn't ashamed of being a woman.

I often think I would have disliked Ceil—at least at times. My mother. I imagine the lunatic and pitiable arrogance, the linguistic drunkenness of my mother on her bed of language and anathema.

I was her child—her infant, really—and the most important thing in her life, she said, but never to the exclusion of her rising in the world or the operations of her will.

In my dreams at night, often the people of a small town crowd around the white-painted wooden farmhouse, carrying torches, to celebrate my election, my revealed glory of destiny; if they applaud or cheer too loudly, I awake and leave them behind in the dream that is a lost planet, a wandering asteroid from which they cannot escape. My mother's dreams and her life were of her election. As in most lives, there is quiet in it, but not often.

Ceil's pride kept her from making friends; friends would have preserved her life but altered the workings and turns of her mind. "She was comfortable only with people who worked for her; she had to be the best; she had great pride in her mind; she thought she knew everything."

Ceil dresses herself in her efforts and her decisions.

Your mother was cursed by your grandfather if she should ever stop being Jewish: look, not just Jewish, strict, you know what I mean—you know what I mean by strict? I don't know if I have the wherewithal to tell you the story if you don't make an effort to understand it on your own; he said she was supposed to die in a bad way if she wasn't a Jew just the way he was, the way he said Jews should be; you know what people are like who have those kinds of minds, don't you? Well, Ceil got taken ill, and she said it was because she wasn't a Jew any more that her father would let in his house.

Now I want to switch to another woman's voice, away from Lila—not a woman I know well. *You want to hear? Mostly, men don't want to know. My mother went to see Ceil in the hospital when she was dying, she went every day, even when Ceil couldn't speak; she said it was good for her* ⌈edifying for her mother: the nobility, the piety, the strength in suffering]—*but maybe not. There's truth in those old things, but how can you tell? Everybody dies anyway. Maybe she didn't keep it up, Ceil, but she had a lot of dignity. She liked God, you know, better than people—maybe except for you. She said she owed it to God. She said she had no right to complain. I don't know if I understood it. She had one sister here, and the sister didn't like her children; they were too American, they weren't good to her—you know how some young people are—and she was afraid they were no good. Ceil told me in confidence that her sister was nothing special: She was a stupid woman and greedy and not very nice. Ceil was different; she talked different; she looked at things different. Her sister hacked herself up with a meat cleaver. You know, it's funny how many suicides I know about. People hide it from children, you know. She made sure no one was in the house; she sent all the children to the movies. Ceil's sister was twenty years older than her. I think there was a curse on her, too. She took the cleaver and she chopped up everything—all her furniture and all her clothes, everything, handkerchiefs and stockings. And then she hit herself over and over, over and over—are you sure you want to hear this—until she was dead. Then Ceil had been having trouble with Max, and she did something she was ashamed of; it was the abortion, but she did it to herself with the help of a Frenchwoman who knew her. And Ceil got a little sick; it was nothing bad, but she went to her sister's funeral and sat shiva and she took you with her, and she said to me that the voice of her father was in that room and she tried not to listen. Ceil had a lot of money in the bank, a lot of money, and she loved you, it was nice to see. She didn't want to die, I promise you that. When she was sick, she said you would feel she ran out on you. A woman is always wrong. I was lucky. It never got so serious for me I* couldn't laugh. Oh, maybe once or twice I thought I would die from it. I wanted to go be in an asylum, but it wasn't my children who saved me. They take, they don't give. She said who would ever give you now what she did, what a mother gives, for no good reason, who would take care of a child like a mother. A woman has her own children or she is ignorant. How can you let a mother go when you're that little and then you have to take what you can get—it's a terrible story, as I said—but she got ill, it was in her soul, she was disgusted with all of us—it happens to a lot of women. She didn't give in right away; the doctors said she would die in a week, but she lived on six months because of you—in pain that was terrible. It couldn't even be God's anger, it was so terrible; it came from the Devil, she said, and the drugs weren't strong enough to touch it. It's terrible when nothing can help. She stank from an infection so bad it made people throw up—it made her sick, her own stench. It was like something out of Hell. They put her on a floor where everyone was dying. You know how doctors run away when they can't help you. And it got worse and worse and worse. She lay there and she plotted to find someone to save you. And to tell you the truth, she didn't want Lila to have you—she didn't like Lila at all; Lila is trash, she said—but when Lila brought you to see her and you were better than you'd been and Lila had on her diamonds and a lot of perfume and you liked her, Ceil said it was better maybe you were saved, no matter what, no matter who it was—even someone, practically a Gentile whore, like Lila: Ceil talked like a rabbi, very strict. She said Lila wasn't as bad as some people thought. Lila was brave. No one could tell Lila what to do. Lila brought you to your mother and she put you in your mother's arms, and you cried when she held you; you can't blame yourself: It was horrible; you knew your mother *only when she was well, a strong woman like that and here is this bag of bones, this woman who prays in a crazy way, and she is crazy with worry about you; and she prayed you'd live and be all right and do something for the Jews. You cried and you turned and you held your arms out to Lila. I'll tell you the truth, it killed Ceil, but she wasn't surprised—she said to me it's easy to die, it was hard to live, I want to die now, and she died that night. Don't blame yourself. The only thing she asked me to tell you is to tell you to remember her.*

I remember her. I hate Jews.

No. I don't really remember her and I don't hate Jews.

In the tormented and torn silence of certain dreams—in the night court of my sleep—sometimes words, like fingers, move and knead and shape the tableaux: shadowy lives in night streets. There is a pearly strangeness to the light. Love and children appear as if in daylight, but it is always a sleeping city, on steep hills, with banked fires and ghosts lying in the streets in the dully reflectant gray light of a useless significance.

I do not believe there was any justice in Ceil's life.

LILA

My protagonists are my mother's voice and the mind I had when I was thirteen.

I was supposed to have a good mind—that supposition was a somewhat mysterious and even unlikely thing. I was physically tough, and active, troublesome to others, in mischief or near delinquency at times and conceit and one thing and another (often I was no trouble at all, however); and I composed no symphonies, did not write poetry, or perform feats of mathematical wizardry. No one in particular trusted my memory since each person remembered differently, or not at all, events I remembered in a way which even in its listing of facts, of actions, was an interpretation; someone would say, "That's impossible—it couldn't have happened like that—I don't do those things—you must be wrong."

But I did well in school and seemed to be peculiarly able to learn what the teacher said—I never mastered a subject, though—and there was the idiotic testimony of those peculiar witnesses, I.Q. tests: Those scores invented me.

Those scores were a decisive piece of destiny in that they affected the way people treated you and regarded you; they determined your authority; and if you spoke oddly, they argued in favor of your sanity. But it was as easy to say and there was much evidence that I was stupid, in every way or in some ways, or as my mother said in exasperation "in the ways that count."

I am only equivocally Wiley Silenowicz. I was adopted when I was two in the month following my real mother's death, and Wiley was a name casually chosen by S. L. Silenowicz because it sounded like Isaac, the name I'd had with my real mother. I was told in various ways over a number of years, and I suppose it's true, that my real father blamed me because I became ill at my mother's death and cried and didn't trust him: I had been my mother's favorite; he kept my brother, who was older than me, and more or less sold me to the Silenowiczes for three hundred and fifty dollars and the promise of a job in another town. I saw my brother once a year, and he told me I was lucky to be adopted. I never told him or anyone else what went on at the Silenowiczes'.

Silenowicz, I learned, is a Polish corruption of a Russian name, originally Byzantine, meaning *Silenus*. Wiley was chosen to conceal my original name, Isaac. To what extent Wiley Silenowicz is a real name is something I have never been able to decide. No decision on the matter makes me comfortable. It's the name I ended with.

In 1943, in the middle of the Second World War, I was thirteen. Thirteen is an age that gives rise to dramas: It is a prison cell of an age, closed off from childhood by the onset of sexual capacity and set apart from the life one is yet to have by a remainder of innocence. Of course, that remainder does not last long. Responsibility and Conscience,

mistaken or not, come to announce that we are to be identi-
fied from then on by what we do to other people: They
free us from limitations—and from innocence—and bind us
into a new condition.

I do not think you should be required to give sympathy.
In rhetoric and in the beauty of extreme feeling, we confer
sympathy always, but in most of life we do quite otherwise,
and I want to keep that perspective. The Silenowiczes were
a family that disasters had pretty completely broken. My
father was in his early forties and had blood pressure so
high the doctors said it was a miracle he was alive. He listened to himself all the time, to the physiological tides in
him; at any moment he could have a stroke, suffer a blood
clot, and pass into a coma: This had happened to him six
times so far; people said, "Sam Silenowicz has the constitu-
tion of a horse." He was not happy with a miracle that was
so temporary. And my mother had been operated on for
cancer, breast cancer: That is, there'd been one operation
and some careful optimism, and then a second operation
and there was nothing left to remove and no optimism at
all. She was forty-five or so. My mother and father were
both dying. There was almost no end to the grossness of
our circumstances. There had been money but there was no
money now. We lived on handouts from relatives who
could not bring themselves to visit us. I used to make jokes
with my parents about what was happening, to show them
I wasn't horrified, and for a while my parents were grateful
for that, but then they found my jokes irritating in the light
of what they were suffering, and I felt, belatedly, the cheap-
ness of my attitude. My mother was at home, not bedridden
but housebound; she said to my father such things as,

"Whether you're sick or not, I have to have money, Sam; I'm not getting the best medical treatment; Sam, you're my husband: You're supposed to see to it that I have money." S. L. Silenowicz signed himself into a Veterans Hospital where the treatment was free, so she could have what money there was and so he could get away from her. I was in ninth grade and went to Ward Junior High School.

We lived in University City, U. City, or Jew City—the population then was perhaps thirty-five percent Jewish; the percentage is higher now. St. Louis swells out like a gall on the Mississippi River. On the western edge of St. Louis, along with Clayton, Kirkwood, Normandy, Webster Groves, is U. City. The Atlantic Ocean is maybe a thousand miles away, the Pacific a greater distance. The Gulf of Mexico is perhaps seven hundred miles away, the Arctic Ocean farther. St. Louis is an island of metropolis in a sea of land. As Moscow is. But a sea of Protestant farmers. Republican small towns. A sea then of mortgaged farms.

It used to give me a crawling feeling of something profound and hidden that neither S. L. nor Lila Silenowicz had been born in the twentieth century. They had been born in years numerically far away from me and historically unfamiliar. We'd never gotten as far as 1898 in a history course. S.L. had been born in Texas, Lila in Illinois, both in small towns. S.L. spoke once or twice of unpaved streets and his mother's bitter concern about dust and her furniture, her curtains; I had the impression his mother never opened the windows in her house: there were Jewish houses sealed like that. Lila said in front of company (before she was ill), "I remember when there weren't telephones. I can remember when everybody still had horses; they made a nice sound walking in the street."

Both S.L. and Lila had immigrant parents who'd made money but hadn't become rich. Both S.L. and Lila had quit college. S.L. his first week or first day, Lila in her second year; both their mothers were famous for being formidable, as battle-axes; both S.L. and Lila believed in being more American than anyone; both despised most Protestants (as naïvely religious, murderously competitive, and unable to have a good time) and all Catholics (as superstitious, literally crazy, and lower class). They were good-looking, small-town people, provincially glamorous, vaudeville-and-movie instructed, to some extent stunned, culturally stunned, liberated ghetto Jews loose and unprotected in the various American decades and milieus in which they lived at one time or another—I don't know that I know enough to say these things about them.

I loved my mother. But that is an evasion. I loved my mother: How much did I love Lila Horowitz? Lila Silenowicz, to give her her married name. I don't think I loved her much—but I mean the *I* that was a thirteen-year-old boy and not consciously her son. All the boys I knew had two selves like that. For us there were two orders of knowledge—of things known and unknown—and two orders of persecution.

S.L. and Lila had not been kind in the essential ways to me—they were perhaps too egocentric to be kind enough to anyone, even to each other. At times, I did not think they were so bad. At times, I did. My mind was largely formed by U. City; my manners derived from the six or seven mansions on a high ridge, the three or four walled and gated neighborhoods of somewhat sternly genteel houses, the neighborhoods of almost all kinds of trim, well-taken-care-of small houses, of even very small houses with sharp gables and fanciful stonework, houses a door and two windows wide with small, neat lawns; and from districts of two-family houses, streets of apartment houses—we lived in an apartment house—from rows of trees, the branches of which met over the streets, from the scattered vacant lots, the unbuilt-on fields, the woods, and the enormous and architecturally grandiose schools.

Every afternoon without stopping to talk to anyone I left school at a lope, sometimes even sprinting up Kingsland Avenue. The suspense, the depression were worst on rainy days. I kept trying to have the right feelings. What I usually managed to feel was a premature grief, a willed concern, and an amateur's desire to be of help any way I could.

It was surprising to my parents and other people that I hadn't had a nervous breakdown.

I spent hours sitting home alone with my mother. At that time no one telephoned her or came to see her. The women she had considered friends had been kind for a while, but it was wartime and my mother's situation did not command the pity it perhaps would have in peacetime. Perhaps my mother had never actually been a friend to the women who did not come to see her: My mother had been in the habit of revising her visiting list upward. But she said she'd been "close" to those other women and that they ought to show respect for her as the ex-treasurer of the Jewish Consumptive Relief Society. She wanted those women to telephone and come and be present at her tragedy. From time to time she'd make trouble: She'd call one of them and remind her how she had voted for her in this or that club election or had given her a lift downtown when she had a car and the other woman hadn't. She told the women she knew they were hardhearted and selfish and would know someday what it was to be sick and to discover what their friends were like. She said still angrier things to her sister and her own daughter (her daughter by birth was ten years older than I was) and her brothers. She had been the good-looking one and in some respects the center of her family, and her physical conceit was unaltered; she had no use for compromised admiration. She preferred nothing. She had been a passionate gameswoman, a gambler: Seating herself at a game table, she had always said, "Let's play for enough to make it interesting."

People said of her that she was a screamer but actually she didn't scream very loudly; she hadn't that much physical force. What she did was get your attention; she would ask you questions in a slightly high-pitched pushy voice that almost made you laugh, but if you were drawn to listen to her, once you were attentive and showed you were, her voice would lose every attribute of sociability, it would become strained and naked of any attempt to please or be acceptable; it would be utterly appalling; and what she said would lodge in the center of your attention and be the truth you had to live with until you could persuade yourself she was crazy, that is, irresponsible and perhaps criminal in her way.

To go see my father in the hospital meant you rode buses and streetcars for three hours to get there; you rode two streetcar lines from end to end; and then at the end of the second line you took a city bus to the end of *its* line and then a gray Army bus that went through a woods to the hospital which stood beside the Mississippi. My father thought it was absurd for me to do that. He said, "I don't need anything—sickness doesn't deserve your notice—go have a good time." To force me to stop being polite, he practiced a kind of strike and would not let me make conversation; he would only say, "You ought to be outdoors." My mother said of my father, "We can't just let him die." Sometimes I thought we could. And sometimes I thought we couldn't. If it had mattered to my father more and not been so much a matter of what I thought I ought to do, it would have been different. He was generous in being willing to die alone and not make any fuss, but I would have preferred him to make a great fuss. When he wouldn't talk, I would go outside; I would stand and gaze at the racing Mississippi, at the eddies, boilings, and racings, at the currents that sometimes curled one above the other and stayed separate although they were water, and I would feel an utter contentment that anything should be that tremendous, that strong, that fierce. I liked loud music, too. I often felt I had already begun to die. I felt I could swim across the Mississippi—that was sheer megalomania: No one even fished in the shallows because of the logs in the river, the entire uprooted whirling trees that could clobber you, carry you under; you would drown. But I thought I could make it across. I wanted my father to recognize the force in me and give it his approval. But he had come to the state where he thought people and what they did and what they wanted were stupid and evil and the sooner we all died the better —in that, he was not unlike Schopenhauer or the Christian Apologists. I am arguing that there was an element of grace in his defeatism. He said that we were all fools, tricked and cheated by everything; whatever we cared about was in the end a cheat, he said. I couldn't wish him dead as he told me I should, but when I wished he'd live it seemed childish and selfish.

Sometimes my father came home for weekends—the hospital made him, I think (letting him lie in bed was letting him commit suicide), but sometimes he did it to see me, to save me from Lila. Neither S.L. nor Lila liked the lights to be on; they moved around the apartment in the shadows and accused each other of being old and sick and selfish, of being irresponsible, of being ugly.

It seemed to me to be wrong to argue that I should have had a happier home and parents who weren't dying: I didn't have a happier home and parents who weren't dying; and it would have been limitlessly cruel to S.L. and Lila, I thought, and emotionally unendurable for me to begin to regret my luck, or theirs. The disparity between what people said life was and what I knew it to be unnerved me at times, but I swore that nothing would ever make me say life should be anything. . . . Yet it seemed to me that I was being done in in that household, by those circumstances.

Who was I? I came from—by blood, I mean—a long line of magic-working rabbis, men supposedly able to impose and lift curses, rabbis known for their great height and temperament: They were easily infuriated, often rhapsodic men.

On the other side I was descended from supposedly a

thousand years or more of Talmudic scholars—men who never worked but only studied. Their families, their children too, had to tend and support them. They were known for their inflexible contempt for humanity and their conceit; they pursued an accumulation of knowledge of the Unspeakable—that is to say, of God.

I didn't like the way they sounded either. In both lines, the children were often rebellious and ran away and nothing more was heard of them: My real father had refused to learn to read and write; he had been a semi-professional gambler, a brawler, a drunk, a prizefighter before settling down to be a junkman. He shouted when he spoke; he wasn't very clean. Only one or two in each generation had ever been godly and carried on the rabbinical or scholarly line, the line of superiority and worth. Supposedly I was in that line. This was more important to Lila than it was to me; she was aware of it; it had meaning to her. Lila said, "If we're good and don't lie, if you pray for me, maybe God will make Sam and me well—it can't hurt to try."

We really didn't know what to do or how to act. Some people, more ardently Jewish than we were, said God was punishing S.L. and Lila for not being better Jews. My real relatives said S.L. and Lila were being punished for not bringing me up as a rabbi, or a Jewish scholar, a pillar of Judaism. "I don't think the Jews are the chosen people," S.L. would say, "and if they are, it doesn't look as if they were chosen for anything good." He said, "What the world doesn't need is another rabbi." At school, the resident psychologist asked my classmates and me to write a short paper about our home life, and I wrote, *It is our wont to have intelligent discussions after dinner about serious issues of the day.* The psychologist congratulated Lila on running a wonderful home from her sickbed, and Lila said to me, "Thank you for what you did for me—thank you for lying." Maybe I didn't do it for her but to see what I could get away with, what I could pass as. But in a way I was sincere. Life at home was concerned with serious questions. But in a way I wasn't ever sincere. I was willing to practice any number of impostures. I never referred to Lila as my *adopted* mother, only as my mother. I had a face that leaked information. I tried to be carefully inexpressive except to show concern toward Lila and S.L. I forgave everyone everything they did. I understood that everyone had the right to do and think as they did even if it harmed me or made me hate them. I was good at games sporadically—then mediocre, then good again, depending on how I regarded myself or on the amount of strain at home. Between moments of drama, I lived inside my new adolescence, surprised that my feet were so far from my head; I rested inside a logy narcissism; I would feel, tug at, and stroke the single, quite long blond hair that grew at the point of my chin. I would look at the new muscle of my right forearm and the vein that meandered across it. It seemed to me that sights did not come to my eyes but that I hurled my sight out like a braided rope and grappled things visually to me; my sight traveled unimaginable distances, up into the universe or into some friend's motives and desires, only to collapse, with boredom, with a failure of will to see to the end, with shyness; it collapsed back inside me: I would go from the sky to inside my own chest. I had friends, good friends, but none understood me or wanted to; if I spoke about the way things were at home, or about my real father, they disbelieved me and then didn't trust me; or if I made them believe, they felt sick, and often they would treat me as someone luckless, an object of charity, and I knew myself to be better than that. So I pitied them first. And got higher grades than they did, and I condescended to them. Lila said to me a number of times, "Don't ever tell anybody what goes on in this house: They won't give you any sympathy; they don't know how—all *they* know is how to run away. . . . Take my advice and lie, say we're all happy, lie a lot if you want to have any kind of life." I did not see how it was possible for such things as curses to exist but it seemed strange I was not ill or half-crazy and my parents were: It didn't seem reasonable that anything except the collapse of their own lives had made S.L. and Lila act as they did or that my adoption had been the means of introducing a curse into the Silenowiczes' existences; but it seemed snotty to be certain. I didn't blame myself exactly; but there was all that pain and misery to be lived with, and it was related to me, to my life; and I couldn't help but take some responsibility for it. I don't think I was neurotic about it.

It seemed to me there were only two social states, tact and madness; and madness was selfish. I fell from a cliff face once, rode my bicycle into a truck on two occasions, was knocked out in a boxing match because I became bored and felt sorry for everyone and lowered my guard and stood there. I wanted to be brave and decent—it seemed braver to be cowardly and more decent not to add to the Sileno-wiczes' list of disasters by having any of my own or even by making an issue of grief or discomfort, but perhaps I was not a very loving person. Perhaps I was self-concerned and a hypocrite, and the sort of person you ought to stay away from, someone like the bastard villains in Shakespeare. Perhaps I just wanted to get out with a whole skin. I thought I kept on going for Lila's and S.L.'s sake but possibly that was a mealymouthed excuse. I didn't know. I tended to rely on whatever audience there was; I figured if they gaped and said, "He's a really good son," I was close to human decency. I was clear in everything I did to make sure the audience understood and could make a good decision about it and me. I was safe in my own life only when there was no one to show off to.

Lila insisted I give her what money I earned. And usually I did so that I would not have to listen to her self-righteous begging and angry persuasiveness. The sums involved were small—five dollars, ten; once it was eighty-nine cents. She had, as a good-looking woman, always tested herself by seeing what she could get from people; hysteria had inflected her old habits and made them grotesque, made her grotesque. No other man was left. No one else at all was left. Not her mother, not her own daughter by blood, not her sister: They ran away from her, moved out of town, hung up if she called. Her isolation was entire except for me. When a nephew of S.L.'s sent me ten dollars for my birthday, Lila said, "I need it, I'm sick, I have terrible expenses. Don't you want to give me the money? Don't you want me to have a little pleasure? I could use a subscription to a good magazine." I used to hide money from her, rolled up in socks, tucked behind photographs in picture frames, but it would always disappear. While I was at school, she would hunt it out: She was ill and housebound, as I said, and there wasn't much for her to do.

Lila never said she was my mother; she never insisted that I had to love her; she asked things of me on the grounds that I was selfish by nature and cold and cut off from human feeling and despised people too much, and she said, "Be manly—that's all I ask." She said, "I don't ask you things that aren't good for you—it's for your own good for you to be kind to me." She would yell at me, "It won't hurt you to help me! You have time for another chance!" Lila yelled, "What do you think it does to me to see you exercising in your room—when I have to die?"

I said, "I don't know. Does it bother you a lot?"

"You're a fool!" she screamed. "Don't make me wish you'd get cancer so you'd know what I'm going through!"

If I ignored her or argued with her, she became violent, and then temper and fright—even the breaths she drew—spoiled the balance of pain and morphine in her; sometimes then she would howl. If I went to her, she would scream, "Go away, don't touch me—you'll hurt me!" It was like having to stand somewhere and watch someone being eaten by wild dogs. I couldn't believe I was seeing such pain. I would stop seeing: I would stand there and be without sight; the bottom of my stomach would drop away; there is a frightening cold shock that comes when you accept the reality of someone else's pain. Twice I was sick, I threw up. But Lila used my regret at her pain as if it were love.

She would start to yell at me at times, and I would lift my arm, my hand, hold them rigidly toward her and say, "Momma, don't . . . don't . . ." She would say, "Then don't make me yell at you. Don't cause me that pain."

It seemed the meagerest imaginable human decency not to be a party to further pain for her. But the list of things she said that caused her pain grew and grew: It upset her to see high spirits in me or a long face; and a neutral look made her think I'd forgotten her predicament; she hated any reference to sports, but she also hated it if I wasn't athletic—it reflected on her if I was a Momma's boy. She hated to talk to me—I was a child—but she had no one else to talk to; that was a humiliation for her. She hated the sight of any pleasure near her, even daydreaming; she suspected that I had some notion of happiness in mind. And she hated it when anyone called me—that was evidence someone had a crush on me. She thought it would help her if I loved no one, was loved by no one, if I accepted help from no one. "How do you think it makes me feel? They don't want to help me, and I'm the one who's dying." She could not bear any mention of the future, any reference especially to my future. "DON'T YOU UNDERSTAND! I WON'T BE HERE!"

Sometimes she would apologize; she would say, "It's not me who says those things; it's the pain. It's not fair for me to have this pain: you don't know what it's like. I can't stand it, Wiley. I'm a fighter."

She said, "Why don't you know how to act so I don't lose my temper? You aggravate me and then I scream at you and it's not good for me. Why don't you understand? What's wrong with you? You're supposed to be so smart but I swear to God you don't understand anything—you're no help to me. Why don't you put yourself in my place? Why don't you coöperate with me?"

She had scorned whatever comfort—or blame—her family had offered her; she said it was incompetent; and she scorned the comfort tendered by the rabbi, who was, she said, "not a *man*—he's silly"; and she suspected the doctors of lying to her, and the treatments they gave her she thought were vile and careless and given with contempt for her. "They burned me," Lila whimpered, "they burned *me*." Her chest was coated with radium burns, with an unpliable, discolored shell. She was held within an enforced, enraged, fearful stiffness. She couldn't take a deep breath. She could only whisper. Her wingspan was so great I could not get near her. I would come home from school and she would be lying on the couch in the living room, whimpering and abject, crying with great carefulness, but angry: She would berate me in whispers: "I hate to tell you this but what you are is selfish, and it's a problem you're going to have all your life, believe me. You don't care if anyone lives or dies. No one is important to you—but you. I would rather go through what I'm going through than be like you." At two in the morning, she came into my room, turned on the ceiling light, and said, "Wake up! Help me. Wiley, wake up." I opened my eyes. I was spread-eagled mentally, like someone half on one side of a high fence, half on the other, but between waking and sleeping. We sometimes had to go to the hospital in the middle of the night. The jumble of words in my head was: *emerging, urgent, murderer, emergency.* I did not call out.

She said, "Look what they've done to me. My God, look what they've done to me." She lowered her nightgown to her waist. The eerie colors of her carapace and the jumble of scars moved into my consciousness like something in a movie advancing toward the camera, filling and overspreading the screen. That gargoylish torso. She spoke first piteously, then ragingly. Her eyes were averted, then she fixed them on me. She was on a flight of emotion, a drug passage, but I did not think of that: I felt her emotion like batwings, leathery and foreign, filling the room; and I felt her animosity. It was directed at me, but at moments it was not and I was merely the only consciousness available to her to trespass upon. She said, "I scratched myself while I slept—look, there's blood."

She had not made me cry since I was a child; I had not let her; nothing had ever made me scream except dreams I'd had that my first mother was not dead but was returning. Certain figures of speech are worn smooth but accurate: I was racked; everything was breaking; I was about to break.

I shouted, "Stop it."

She said enraged, "Am I bothering you? Are you complaining about me? Do you know what I'm suffering?"

I said, "No." Then I said—I couldn't think of anything sensible—"It doesn't look so bad, Momma."

She said, "What's wrong with you? Why do you talk stupidly?" Locks of hair trailed over her face. She said, "No one wants to touch me."

I raised my eyebrows and stuck my head forward and jerked it in a single nod, a gesture boys used then for OK when they weren't too pleased, and I climbed out of bed. My mother told me at breakfast the next day not to mind what she had done, it had been the drug in her that made her do what she did; the batwings of her drug flight seemed when I stood up to fold back, to retreat inside her: she was not so terrifying. Merely unlikable. And sickening. I put my arms around her and said, "See. I can hug you."

She let out a small scream. "You're hurting me."

"OK, but now go back to bed, Momma. You need your sleep."

"I can't sleep, why don't you want to kill the doctor for what he's done to me . . ."

She said for weeks, whenever she was drugged, "If I was a man, I'd be willing to be hanged for killing a man who did this to a woman I loved."

She'd had five years of various illnesses and now cancer and she still wasn't dead.

I would come home from school to the shadowy house, the curtains drawn and no lights on, or perhaps one, and she would be roaming barefooted with wisps of her hair sticking out and her robe lopsided and coming open; when I stood there, flushed with hurrying, and asked, "Momma, is it worse?" or whatever, she would look at me with pinched-face insanity and it would chill me. She would shout, "What do you mean, is it worse? Don't you know yet what's happened to me? What else can it be but worse! What's wrong with you? You're more of my punishment, you're helping to kill me, do you think I'm made of iron? You come in here and want me to act like your valentine! I don't need any more of your I-don't-know-what! You're driving me crazy, do you hear me? On top of everything else, you're driving me out of my mind."

Feelings as they occur are experienced as if they were episodes in Kafka, overloaded with hints of meaning that reek of eternity and the inexplicable and that suggest your dying—always your dying—at the hands of a murderousness in events if you are not immediately soothed, if everything is not explained at once. It is your own selfishness or shamefulness, or someone else's or perhaps something in fate itself that is the murderer; or what kills is the proof that your pain is minor and is the responsibility of someone who does not care. I didn't know why I couldn't shrug off what she did and said; I didn't blame her; I even admired her when I didn't have to face her; but I did not see why these things had to happen, why she had to say these things. I think it mattered to her what I felt. That is, if I came in and said, "Hello, Momma," she would demand, "Is that all you can say? I'm in *pain*. Don't you care? My God, my God, what kind of selfish person are you? I can't stand it."

If I said, "Hello, Momma, how is your pain?" she would shriek, "You fool, I don't want to think about it! It was all right for a moment! Look what you've done—you've brought it back. . . . *I don't want to be reminded of my pain all the time!*"

She would yell, "What's wrong with you? Why don't you know how to talk to me! My God, do you think it's easy to die? Oh my God, I don't like this. I don't like what's happening to me! My luck can't be this bad." And then she would start in on me: "Why do you just stand there? Why do you just listen to me! It doesn't do me any good to have you there listening! You don't do anything to help me— what's wrong with you? You think I'm like an animal? Like a worm? You're supposed to be smart, but you don't understand anything, you're no good to me, you were never any good to me. I'd laugh at you, you're so useless to me, but it hurts me to laugh: What good are you to me? Do something for me! Put yourself in my place! Help me! Why don't you help me?"

Sometimes she would say in a horrible voice, "I'll tell you what you are—I'll tell you what everyone is! They're trash! They're all trash! My God, my God, how can my life be like this? I didn't know it would be like this. . . ."

I really did not ever speak to anyone about what went on at home, but one of the teachers at school suggested that I apply for a scholarship to Exeter, so that I could get away from the "tragedy in your home." And get a good education as well. I was secretly hopeful about going to boarding school a thousand miles away. I did not at all mind the thought that I would be poorer and less literate than the boys there. I figured I would be able to be rude and rebellious and could be hateful without upsetting my mother and I could try to get away with things.

I remember the two of us, Lila and me in the shadowy living room: I'm holding some books, some textbooks. She's wearing a short wrap-around housecoat, with a very large print of vile yellow and red flowers with green leaves on a black background. I've just told her casually I can go away to school; I put it that I would not be a burden on her any more or get on her nerves; I told her I did not want to be a burden—I said something like that; that was my attempt at tact. She said, "All right—leave me too—you're just like all the rest. You don't love anyone, you never loved anyone. You didn't even mourn when your real mother died, you don't ever think about her—I'll tell you what you are: you're filth. Go. Get out of here. Move out of here tonight. Pack up and go. I don't need you. No one will ever need you. You're a book, a stick, you're all book learning, you don't know anything about people—if I didn't teach you about people, people would laugh at you all the time, do you hear me?"

I went into another room and I think I was sitting there or maybe I was gathering together the ten or fifteen books I owned, having with a kind of boy's dishonesty I suppose, taken Lila's harangue as permission to leave her, as her saying yes in her way to my going away, my saving myself, when she came in. She'd put on lipstick and a hair ribbon; and her face, which had been twisted up, was half all-right, the lines were pretty much up and down and not crooked; and my heart began to beat sadly for myself—she was going to try to be nice for a little while; she was going to ask me to stay.

After that she seemed to feel I'd proved that I belonged to her; or it had been proved I was a man she could hold near her still. Every day, I came home from school, and Lila fluttered down from her filthy aerie of monstrous solitude and pain: In a flurry of dust and to the beating of leathery wings, she asked me a riddle. Sometimes she threatened me: She'd say, "You'll die in misery too—help me now and maybe God will be good to you." Or she'd say, "You'll end like me if you don't help me!" She'd say it with her face screwed up in fury. She'd say, "Why don't you put yourself in my place and understand what I'm going through." It occurred to me that she really didn't know what she was saying—she was uttering words that sounded to her close to something she really wanted to say; but what she said wasn't what she meant. Maybe what she meant couldn't be said. Or she was being sly because she was greedy and using bluff or a shortcut and partly it was her own mental limitation and ineptness: that is, she couldn't say what she hadn't thought out.

It wasn't enough that I stayed with her and did not go to Exeter. She railed at me, "You're not doing me any good —why don't you go live in the Orphans' Home: That's where heartless people who don't deserve to have a family belong." We both knew that I didn't have to go to the Orphans' Home but maybe neither of us knew what she meant when she demanded I help her. It was queer, the daily confrontations, Lila and me not knowing what she wanted from me or even what the riddle really was that she was asking. She crouched there or seemed to at those moments, in the narrow neck of time between afternoon and evening, between the metaphorical afternoon of her being consigned to death and the evening of her actual dying, and she asked me some Theban riddle while she was blurred with drugs, with rage, and I looked at her and did not know what to do.

But after a while I knew sort of what she was asking: I knew sort of what the riddle was; but I couldn't be sure. I knew it was partly she wanted me to show I loved her in some way that mattered to her, that would be useful; and it was wrong of her to ask, I knew because she was ashamed or afraid when she spoke to me and she averted her eyes, or they would be sightless, unfocused from the morphine. In a way, pity could not make me do anything, or love. The final reasons are always dry ones, are rational and petty: I wanted to do something absolutely straightforward and finally loyal to her, something that would define my life with her in such a way that it would calm her and enable me to be confident and less ashamed in the future and more like other people. And also if I were going to live with her for a while, things had to change; I wanted to know that life for me did not have to be like *this*. Things had to be made bearable for both of us.

It doesn't sound sensible—to make her dying and my being with her bearable. But it is language and habit that make the sense odd. It was clear to me that after a process of fantastic subtraction I was all that was left to her. And for me what with one odd subtraction and another, she was the only parent I had left to me; she was my mother.

I could half see, in the chuffing, truncated kind of thought available to my thirteen-year-old intelligence that the only firm ground for starting was to be literal: She had asked me to put myself in her place. OK. But what did that mean? How could I be a dying, middle-aged woman walking around in a housedress?

I knew I didn't know how to think; I guessed that I had the capacity—just the *capacity*—to think: That capacity was an enormous mystery to me, perhaps as a womb is to a woman. When I tried to think, I wandered in my head but not just in my head; I couldn't sit down physically and be still and think: I had to be in movement and doing something else; and my attention flittered, lit, veered, returned. Almost everyone I knew could *think* better than I could. Whenever I thought anything through, I always became a little angry because I felt I'd had to think it out to reach a point that someone better parented would have known to start with. That is, whenever I thought hard, I felt stupid and underprivileged. I greatly preferred to feel. Thinking for me was always accompanied by resentment, and was in part a defensive, a rude and challenged staring at whatever I was trying to think about; and it was done obstinately and blunderingly—and it humiliated me.

Death, death, I said to myself. I remembered Lila saying, "I don't want to be shut up in a coffin." That was fear and drama: It didn't explain anything. But it did if she wasn't dead yet: I mean I thought that maybe the question was *dying. Dying.* Going toward a coffin. Once when I was little I'd found a horizontal door in the grass next to a house; I had been so small the door had been very hard to lift and to lay down again because my arms were so short; when the door was open, you saw stairs, unexpected in the grass, and there was a smell of damp and it was dark below, and you went down into an orderly place, things on shelves, and the light, the noises, the day itself, the heat of the sun were far away; you were coolly melted; your skin, your name dissolved; you were turned into an openness, into being a mere listening and feeling; the stillness, the damp, the aloneness, the walls of earth, of moist, whitewashed plaster soaked you up, blurred you; you did not have to answer when anyone called you.

And when you fell from your bike, while you were falling, the way everything stopped except the knowledge that pain was coming. The blotting out of voices, the sudden distance of everything, the hope, the conviction almost that this was a dream, the way time drew out, was airy, and nothing was going to happen, and then everything turned to stone again; it was going to happen; the clatter of your bike crashing, your own fall; and then finally you sat up with disbelief and yet with knowledge: you saw your torn pants; you poked at the bleeding abrasions on your elbow that you had to twist your arm to see. You felt terrible but you didn't know yet, you couldn't know everything that had happened to you.

I remembered in pictures, some quite still, some full of motion, none of them rectangular; and what I meant, while it was clear enough to me at first, became liquid and foggy when I tried to establish in words what it was I meant, what it was I now knew; it slid away into a feeling of childishness, of being wrong, of knowing nothing, after all.

Lila wouldn't have those feelings about dying. And my feelings were beside the point and probably wrong even for me. Then my head was blank and I was angry and despairing; but all at once my scalp and neck wrinkled with gooseflesh. I had my first thought about Lila. She wouldn't think in those pictures, and they didn't apply to her because she wouldn't ever think in pictures that way, especially about dying: Dying was a fact. She was factual and pictureless.

Then after that I made what I called an equation: Lila-was-Lila. I meant that Lila was not me and she was really alive.

That made me feel sad and tired and cheated—I resented it that she was real and not me or part of me, that her death wasn't sort of a version of mine. It was going to be too much God-damned work this way.

I went off into "thinking," into an untrained exercise of intellect. I started with xs and ys and Latin phrases. I asked myself what was a person, and, after a while, I came up with: a person is a mind, a body, and an I. The I was not

in the brain, at least not in the way the mind was. The *I* is
what in you most hurts other people—it makes them lonely.
But the mind and body make it up to people for your *I*. The
I was the part that was equal in all men are created equal
and have the same rights to life, liberty, and the pursuit of
happiness. The emotions of the *I* were very different from
the emotions of the body and the mind. When all three
parts of you overlapped, it was what people meant by "the
heart."

Lila's heart. Lila's mind, Lila's body, Lila's *I*.

Inside a family, people have mythologically simple char-
acters—there's the angry one, the bookish one, and so on,
as if everyone were getting ready to be elevated and turned
into a constellation at any moment. Notions of character
were much less mythical once you got outside a family usually. Lila in her family was famous for her anger, but she
had also said of herself a number of times that she had more
life in her than her husband or her mother and sister and
brothers and daughter. It had always made me curious.
What did it mean to have more life in you? She'd never said
I had much life in me, or a little. It seemed to me on reflection Lila had meant her temper. A lot of her temper came
from restlessness and from seeing people and things the
way she did. She'd meant she couldn't sit quietly at home
or believe in things that weren't real. Or be a hypocrite.
She'd meant she was a fighter; active—but she never played
any sport, not any; she was the most unexercised woman I
knew of: she never did housework, never went dancing any
more (I meant before she'd been sick), never swam or
played tennis, never gardened or walked, never carried
groceries—if she shopped she paid a delivery boy to bring

the groceries home for her. She never failed to sleep at night although she complained of sleeping badly—she didn't have so much life she couldn't sleep. She dreamed a lot; she liked to have things happen, a lot every day. She liked to go places, to get dressed up, to get undressed and be slatternly: She was always acting, always busy being someone, performing in a way. Was that the life in her? She insisted that people control their minds and not think too much and she didn't approve of bodies' being too active—she really was mostly interested in the *I: I like to live, I want a good life, you don't know how to live, I know what life is, I know how to live, there's a lot of life in me, I have a lot of life in me.*

I thought these things at various times; they occurred to me over a number of days. My mind wandered into and out of the subject. Preoccupied with it at times, I dropped and broke things or got off the bus at the wrong stop or stumbled on the curbstone, holding my textbooks in one hand, their spines turned upward leaning against my thigh, in the style of a sharp high school boy. Girls at school told me I was looking "a lot more mature."

Every once in a while, I would remember something: Lila saying angrily, "I pushed my brothers, I put every idea they had into their heads, I was somebody in that little town—" (In Illinois.) "People thought I was something, it was me that gave my brothers a name; that's all it takes to win an election, a name. J.J. was mayor, Mose was police commissioner—you don't think it did them some good? And I put them over. They looked *Jewish*—it was *my* looks, me and Sam, Sam was in the American Legion: Believe me, that helped. And it was all my idea. Momma never wanted us to do nothing, Momma thought the Gentiles would kill us if we got to be too outstanding. She was always in Russia in her mind. I was the smartest one—Momma and my brothers weren't as smart as I was. I could always get people to do what I wanted. Who do you think told J.J. what to wear? I taught him how to look like a businessman so he could go into St. Louis and people wouldn't laugh at him. I found him his wife, he owes me a lot. But I have to give him credit, he's the only one who had brains, he's the only one who did anything with what I told him. If you ask me, Mose can't count to fifteen without getting a headache, and Sam was not smart either. Sam was vain: When he went bald I had to fight with him to take off his hat in the house: He did have pretty hair: He was too blond to be a Jew. But everything was a pose with him, he never did anything because it was smart, it was always Sam putting his hand in his pocket and being a big shot—believe me, a lot of women thought he was attractive. But you couldn't talk to Sam, no one could ever talk to Sam, he wouldn't listen, he had his own ideas—ideas! I'm the one to say it, I married him, I made my bed—he was dumb: I had to have the brains for both of us. But good-looking, my God. The first time I saw him I couldn't believe it, he was so good-looking: I didn't think he was Jewish. He was in an officer's uniform. You can imagine. I was never photogenic but I was something to look at, myself. Sam took one look at me and he didn't know if he was coming or going. He cut in on me at a dance and asked me to marry him just like that and he meant it. He meant well. I really wasn't bad-looking: People always told me everything. I was too pretty when I was young to make it in St. Louis—older women ran things in St. Louis—you think I didn't catch on? St. Louis is a good town for a woman when you get older: I know what I'm talking about. I knew the right time to move here. If Sam had been a businessman, we could have caught up with J.J.—we had good chances, people liked me, but Sam didn't go over, he didn't make friends with smart people, he wouldn't take my advice. I should have been the type who could get divorced but I never believed in divorce: It would just be the frying pan into the fire: Marriage is never easy. Listen, I'm smart: I'd've liked to try my luck in Chicago, I've always been outstanding, I've always impressed people. . . ."

It seemed to me from what little I could remember about her when I was little, and before S.L. became ill, that she had interested the people around her. Everyone had looked at her wherever she went and people waited for her to arrive for the excitement to start. And they had been afraid of her too. When she was all dressed up—and even when she wasn't—she often looked glamorous and interesting: She'd worn things like a black suit with wide lapels, very high-heeled black shoes, longish black gloves, a diamond bracelet on the outside of one glove, a fur neckpiece, fox heads biting their tails, a tight-fitting hat with a long feather fastened to it by a red jewel, and a veil drawn over her face; and behind the veil a very red lipsticked mouth.

I hadn't as a child clearly understood what we were to each other. She'd been so different in her moods, she hadn't ever seemed to be one person, to be the same person for long, to be the same person at all. When I was little, I'd been allowed to sit on her bed and watch her get dressed—this had been a privilege awarded me and a kind of joke and thing of affection. She'd been a slightly dumpy, slack-skinned, nervous woman with a wried mouth and eyes muddy with temper. She would arrange a towel around her shoulders and bosom while she sat at a vanity table, and then she would brush her hair; she would beat at her hair with the brush; she would stick out her chin and brace against the force of her brushing. What was wonderful was that as she brushed, a faint life, like a sunrise, would creep into her face—a smoothness; she'd be less wrinkled, less skewed in anger or impatience, in bitterness or exhaustion; a pinkness, very faint, would spread around the line of her hair; her face would not look so ashen then. Part of it was that her hair would begin to shine, part was that her face would reveal an increasing, magical symmetry, part was the life in her eyes, but she became pretty. I would stare at her reflection in the mirror. I had to keep looking at her because if I closed my eyes or ran out of the room, the prettiness would disappear from my head, and then I'd have to run back and look at her. Seated at the vanity table, she'd say things that were strange to me and grown-up (I thought) and private. "I had good coloring when I was young but you know what they say: You don't stay young forever." Or, "I look like a ghost." On the spur of the moment she would change the curve of her eyebrows and the shape of her lips or use another shade of powder and of lipstick: It would be very strained while she did it, she would be intent and bold and willful, like a gambler. God, the hushed niceness of the looks, the romantic, whispery, gentle niceness she would often end with. Sometimes she tried for startlingly dramatic looks and got them or partly got them; sometimes she failed and had to wipe her face clean and redo her hair and start over. She would get, at this point, if things seemed to be working, a blunt, broad, female, and sarcastic excitement, a knowing gaiety, a tough-fibered, angry pleasure and a despair that moved me. If I said, "You're pretty, Momma," she would say in the new voice of her new mood, "Do you think I'm the cat's miaow?" Sometimes she would keep repeating that but in changing, softening voices until she came to a gentle, teasing voice, one as sweet as a lullaby with agreeable and patient inner themes. She was a complete strategist. Sometimes she would sing "Yes, Sir, That's My Baby." As if she were a man and were admiring herself. Sometimes her voice would be quavering and full of half-suffocated, real pleasure, readily amorous or flirtatious. I think she was always the first to be affected by her looks.

Three times that I can think of, when I was alone at home, I sneaked a look into my mother's bureau, at her underwear . . . but also at her jewelry and handkerchiefs and sweaters: I wanted to see what was hidden. Other motives I pass over. Once, and maybe twice, I tried on a nightgown of hers and danced on the bed and saw myself in the bureau mirror. I don't remember feeling that I was like a woman in any way. I can remember moments of wanting to be one, when I was fairly young—to wear a turban and be opinionated and run everything in the house and not ever have to prove myself—but the wish wasn't sexual, so far as I know, or profound or long-lived. It was envy of women having power without having to serve apprenticeships for it. And also it was a daydream about safety and being taken care of and undoing some of the mistakes of having grown to be seven or eight years old: A woman, like a little boy, was a specialist in being loved.

My ignorance about women was considerable—why were women so secretive? I knew my mother and my sister faked just about absolutely everything they did with men, but why? Their temper, their good nature, their unhappiness, their happiness were almost always fake—but why? I didn't understand what the need was for all the fraud.

No man or boy was ever permitted to be outspoken near a woman. In U. City, there weren't too many docile, crushed women or girls; I didn't know any. In U. City, women sought to regulate everyone in everything; they more or less tried to supersede governmental law, instinct, tradition, to correct them and lay down new rules they insisted were the best ones. Nearly everything they wanted from us —to be polite, to sit still, to be considerate, to be protective —was like a dumb drumming of their wanting us to be like women. The rarest thing in a woman was any understanding of the male. And that wasn't asked of them. Women were highly regarded and in U. City it was considered profoundly wicked to be rude to any of them. One simply fled from them, avoided them. Their unjust claims. I mean we respected women as women, whatever they were as people.

I thought about my mother's name, Lila Horowitz Silenowicz, as mine. It seemed intensely silly to be called Lila. Then one day I thought about being a woman called Lila who was all dressed up and then was being pushed head first into a keg of oil. It was unbearable. And disgusting. I thought I had imagined what it was like to be Lila dying, to be a dying woman. I woke the next day from a night's sleep having realized in my sleep I had not imagined my mother's dying at all.

She was in her forties and she had cancer and she had

some twist to her character so that she drove people away. People said she had "a bad mouth"—she was cutting and shrill, demanding, she said true things in full malice. The more I thought about being her, the more masculinely I held myself: Even my thoughts were baritone.

She had an odd trait of never blaming herself, and nothing anyone ever said about her affected her in a way that led her to change. She never listened to my father at all, or to her mother, or her daughter, or her friends. That simmered in my head a few days before it took another shape. I was at football practice. We were running up and down the football field lifting our knees high as we were told. I was afraid of the coach. Suddenly it occurred to me my mother was undisciplinable, ineducable, and independent: She refused to be controlled by sexual pleasure, so far as I could see, or by conventional notions of what was maternal or by what people thought or by their emotional requirements. But it was a queer independence and one of the mind or of the pride: She felt it in her mind: But it wasn't what I'd call independence: She was tied to her family; she couldn't conceive of moving far away; she couldn't bear to be alone; she needed to have someone in love with her: She was independent of the claims of the person in love with her, but she needed the feelings directed at her for her to be independent of something. Time after time, after quarrels with certain friends or with her family, she would say, "I don't care, I don't need them," but she was peculiarly defenseless and *always* let people come back, even if they were just wastes of time and drains on her energy. She couldn't bear to lose anyone. She was like a creature without a shell and without claws and so on—she was rather a soft person—and she sort of with her mind or mother-wit made a shell and claws, and needed, and wanted, and pursued people, men and women, who would be part of her—of her equipment—who would care about her and outfit her and help her. She fawned on such people to get them to like her until she felt, correctly or paranoiacally, that they didn't care about her, that they had failed her; then she would assail them behind their back for practice and when the scurrility was polished she'd deliver it to their faces.

It seemed hot and airless even to begin to work on imagining what it was like to be my mother.

One thing I did not know then but half know now was that I was not independent of her. I thought then I did not love her exactly; she struck me as having no aptitude for happiness, and so there was no point in being attached to her or having a lot of feeling about her—she'd only use it against me. I knew she was no mother in any conventional sense; she herself often said as much; but the fact that she was such a terrible mother made me feel aristocratic and amused as well as tired me: I saw other mothers charging around half destroying their kids, crippling them, blinding them, and I felt protective toward my mother—this was a dry, adolescently sarcastic, helpless feeling, almost part of my sense of humor, my sense of aristocracy, if I can call it that, this being protective toward her. Also, I figured that when I was an infant someone had been kind to me: I was comparatively strong physically, and surprisingly unfrightened of things, and I gave credit for this to Lila.

But I know now I was frightened of a lot of things; I just didn't pay much attention to the fright. My ignorance, my character scared me. I could hide behind taking care of her.

I leaned on the fact of having her near me; her presence, having to take care of her, supplied an answer to a lot of questions, supplied a shape. I didn't have to know who I was. Girls pushed me around a lot: There was a dim shadowy hysteria in me about that. I didn't often feel it, but I needed and resented Lila. I thought I was objective and emotionless and so on, but I wasn't: She was important to me.

I had noticed that she never blamed herself, but then I saw that she never blamed any woman much, even women she was angry with; she'd say such-and-such a woman was selfish and a lousy friend and that she never wanted to see her again but my mother really launched diatribes only against men. She had a brother who'd become rich, and she said he was ruled by his wife, that his wife kept this brother from being nice to Lila, but what Momma did was stop speaking to her brother and she went on being friends with her sister-in-law.

I couldn't see how Momma managed this presumption of sinlessness in women. Finally I worked it out that she felt women were in an unfair situation, and had to do what they did. She never thought women were bound by honor or by any of the things men were bound by. At one point, enraptured with my daring, I wondered if my mother were basically a lesbian. But then it seemed to me she was much more afraid of women than she was of men, so maybe she was merely trying to get along with other women who were the real danger and so on.

She never forgave, never forgot anything I said to her in anger—she remembered rudenesses I'd committed when I was four years old. But she said that what *she* said didn't matter and didn't mean anything. The same with complaints; she went on and on about how grim life was and how terrible most people were but if I even so much as said that school was dull, she said, "Be a man—don't complain."

I couldn't figure out that one-sidedness: How did she expect not to irritate me, not to bore me? Then suddenly I had an inspiration which maybe had nothing to do with the truth, but I could imagine she might want to be independent of absolutely everything, even of having to be fair in the most minor way. . . .

My poor mother's freedom. She was utterly wretched, and at this point in her life she screamed most of the time rather than spoke. "I have no life. . . . Why did this happen to me. . . ." And, "My brothers are filth. . . ." And so on.

One day she was ranting about one of her brothers, "He used to be in love with me but now he won't come near me because I'm ugly and sick—" and it occurred to me she was enraged—and amazed—to discover selfishness in anyone except her. No one had the right to be selfish except Lila.

She remembered everything she had ever done as having been a favor for someone. And this wasn't just madness, although I thought so at first; it was her cold judgment of how life operated: It was her estimate of what she was worth. Or a bluff. She thought or hoped she was smarter and prettier and more realistic than anyone.

To watch somebody and think about them is in a way to begin to have the possibility of becoming them.

It seemed to me I could see certain ways we were already alike and that I had never noticed before. I had never noticed that I had almost no pity for what men suffered—in a war, say; I didn't care if men got hurt, or if I hurt boys in a fight, so I was always more comfortable with men than with women. And I caught sight of something in me I hadn't admitted to consciousness but it was that I judged all the time how well I was being taken care of, even while thinking I did not ask to be taken care of at all. And she was like that. She thought pain belonged to women; she did not like men who suffered; she thought suffering in men was effeminate. She didn't think men deserved help: She was a woman and too exposed; she had to be taken care of first. I tried to imagine a conscious mind in which all this would seem sensible and obvious.

I heard a woman say, "It's easy for me to be nice—I have a husband who is good to me. . . ."

It was terrifying to contemplate the predicament hinted at in such a speech.

I could believe a lot of what my mother was was what had been done to her.

She said to me once, "I would have been happy married to a gangster." I knew people did not always say what they meant: They uttered words that seemed to make the idea in their heads audible but often the sentence said nothing or said the opposite to anyone outside their heads who did not know all the connections. Partly because the idea was defective, but more often because in simple egotism and folly one could say, especially if one were a woman, "Why don't you understand me?" and never think about the problem of having to make oneself clear. Men had to make themselves clear in order to run businesses and to act as judges, but in order to be clear they said less and less: They standardized their speeches. Or were tricky or—But anyway when my mother said something it seemed easiest to take her literally because the literal meaning would cover more of her intention than any interpretive reading would. She often became very angry with me for taking her literally, but since no one else understood her at all, ever, I thought my system was the best possible, and also, by taking her literally, I could control her a little.

When she said she would have been happy with a gangster, it was hard to know what she meant: Did she need violence, did she want a man who could be violent because of how he would act toward her, or because of the way he'd act toward other people? I guessed she wanted someone to be tough toward the world, who would be her fists, who would be no fool, and who, busy with his own life, would give her a certain freedom. My mother did not like needing anyone—"If you don't need anybody, you don't get hurt" —but she needed people all the time. She said of my real mother, "She was brave—she went where she wanted to go, she would go alone, she didn't need anyone, I don't know where she got the strength, but she could stand alone. I envied her, I wanted to be like her. I wanted to adopt you because I thought you would be like her."

I thought, without much confidence, that women were held under the constraint of social custom more than men were: Almost all of *civilization* had to do with the protection and restraint of women; but *that* seemed to be true of men too. My mother lived a half-fantasy of being tough, she was verbally tough: a failed adventurer. She wanted to have her own soul and to stand outside the law: She thought she could be independent if only she had a little help. My mother was willing, up to a point, to blaspheme, to try to defraud God.

Then, more and more, it seemed to me my mother hated all connections; even her bones did not seem to be fastened to each other, I noticed; my mother was soft, fluid, sea-y, a sea-y creature. What harrowed her most was the failure of her maneuvers, of her adaptations, her lack of success. It seemed to *me* that her illness was an experience, an act of destiny outside the whole set of things that made up that part of life where you were a success or failure. Will and charm and tactics could manage just so much—then you had to believe in God or luck or both, which led you into theological corruption of a very sickening kind (I could not believe God would help you make money). They were two different orders of experience, but my mother thought they were one. She thought your luck as far as having looks was part of the other, even though she said, "Anyone can be good-looking—you have to try, you have to carry yourself right, sometimes ugly people are the best-looking of all. . . ." She was generous enough to admit of some women, "I was much prettier than her once but she's outdistanced me: She knows how to dress, she's taken care of herself. . . ."

Riding on the bus I tried to imagine myself—briefly— a loose-fleshed, loose-boned soft-looking woman like my mother with her coarse ambitiousness and soulful public manner (when she wasn't being shrill) and the exigent fear of defeat that went with what she was. . . . I did it sort of absently, almost half-drowsing, I thought it was so, well, dull, or unilluminating. But suddenly I experienced an extraordinary vertigo, and a feeling of nausea, and I stopped quickly.

I didn't know if I'd felt sick because I was doing something I shouldn't do—I mean I started with that notion, and it was only a day or so later I thought maybe the nausea had gone with imagining defeat. So far as I knew, I did not mind defeat—defeat hurt, but it offered an excuse for being indulgent and sexual and so on.

I didn't even conceive of total defeat. Being a hobo would be a fate, getting meningitis and dying, being a homosexual, a drunk, a lifelong shoe salesman would be a fate, maybe even amusing. None of that really frightened me. I wondered if it was the war that had done this to me or if I'd been cheated out of a certain middle-classness. Maybe it was that in never having been given much by Lila I'd come not to expect much in general, or maybe I just didn't fear failure properly, or it had to do with being masculine.

So I had to *imagine* what it would be like to really hate failure. I worked out a stupid idea that Lila needed family, social position, charm, looks, clothes, or she couldn't begin to have adventures; something that didn't require those things was not a real adventure. She maybe needed those things as someone might need a hearing aid or glasses or a tractor or a car: A woman deprived of them was deaf, blind, reduced to trudging hopelessly along.

I was not obsessed with understanding my mother; I worked on this when I had the time.

I sometimes imagined myself in combat conditions, I tried to imagine myself undergoing humiliations, deprivations. It was a matter of pride not to run away from painful thoughts.

I knew my mother had never made an imaginative leap into my life or into any man's life; she'd said so: "I know nothing about being a boy. . . ." She'd said to my father, "I know nothing about being a man. . . ." She did not like movies that were about men. She never asked me to tell her about myself. Perhaps she was defiant because Jewish women were supposed to be respectful toward men—I couldn't handle that thought—but it seemed to me *very* clear she was interested only in her own fate as a woman. She thought everyone dealt in ruses, in subterfuge, but that she did it best. Her world bewildered me. I assumed she did not love me. I did not know to what extent I loved her. I saw that my insensitivity to her, as long as she behaved the way she did, was the only thing that made it possible for me to be halfway decent to her. If I reacted to her directly, I would become a major figure in the drama, and it would become clear she was a terrible pain in the neck, a child, and a fool. She thought if I became sensitive to her I would be struck with admiration for her in what she was going through, as once men had fallen in love with her at first sight. But I knew that would not happen. The depth of pain she suffered did not make her beautiful, could not make her beautiful: What she did, how she acted was the only thing that could make her beautiful. Maybe once sheer physical glory had made her redoubtable but I figured she'd had to work on her looks. There was nothing you could be without effort except catatonic. If I became sensitive to her and she was careless of me, I would not care if she died.

Obviously, between her and me there were two different minds and sensibilities and kinds of judgment operating: She wanted to control my mind—but without taking responsibility for it. She wanted to ascribe not a general value but a specifically masculine value to my being sympathetic toward her pain. It seemed to me she did not have that right because she had not carried out any specifically feminine side to our relationship, to any bargain. I mean she was working a swindle. She was also trying to help me. She wanted her condition considered a heroic, serious event, but I had nearly died twice in my childhood, and both times she had said, "Be brave." She had experienced no discomfort, only "aggravation" when I'd been ill—"I'm not good at illness," she'd said. You couldn't hold the past against people, but on the other hand what other contract did you have with anyone except that past?

My mother did not expect gentleness from people on the whole, but when she was desperate she wept because there was no gentleness in anyone near her. She preferred to go to Catholic hospitals when she was ill because of the nuns: They forgave her over and over. She lied to them and told them she would convert, and then she took it back and said God would punish her if she stopped being Jewish. She screamed and railed at people but the nuns always forgave her. "They're good—they understand women," she said. She whispered, "I'm a terrible person but they don't mind."

She said she could not bear it when people came near her and thought of themselves.

I did not do anything merely in order to be good to her. I decided to fiddle around with being—with being a little taken advantage of. I did it as a profanation, as a gesture of contempt for the suburb and toward people who pitied Lila; I did it as an exercise in doing something illicit and foul, as an exercise in risk-taking and general perversity. I figured, well, what the hell, why not do it, what did I have to lose? I was probably already wrecked and I'd probably be killed in the war besides.

I trained myself to listen to her talk about how she felt;

I didn't wince or lose my appetite when she went on and on about what she was going through. Actually I was losing weight and having nightmares, but I'd get up in the middle of the night and do pushups so I'd sleep and look healthy the next day. I wanted her to know I accepted what she went through as "normal."

She could of course describe only with limited skill, thank God, her pain.

"I have a burning—it begins here—" Her eyes would fill with tears "—and then it goes to *here!*" And she would start to tremble. "I want to kill everybody," she would whisper, "I become a terrible person—" (She'd been terrible before, though.) "I don't know what to do. Why is this happening to me?"

She said, "If I believed in Heaven, if I thought I could go there and see my father and my sister Sarah—they were always good to me—I wouldn't be so afraid." She said, "It always seemed to me the good died young but I wasn't good and I'm dying young."

I was much too shy to imagine myself a woman physically, in exact detail, cleft and breasted.

My mother's room had a wallpaper of roses, large roses, six or seven inches across, set quite close together. One day, sitting with her in a chair by her bed, it occurred to me she could not bear any situation in which she could not cheat. What she said was "I don't know what good morphine is! It doesn't help enough—I can't get away with anything." She may have meant *from* anything but I took her meaning the other thing. She also said, "If I pray it doesn't help, the pain doesn't stop."

"Do you believe in God, Momma?"

"I don't know—why doesn't He help me?"

"You're supposed to praise Him whether you're in pain or not."

"That's unfair."

"Well, we're not supposed to judge *Him*."

"I don't want a God like that," she said.

"If you believed what the Catholics believed, you could pray to the Virgin Mary."

"No woman made this world. I couldn't pray to a woman."

Much of her restlessness and agony came from comparing what the movies said life was and death was and what pain was for women with what she actually had to confront in her life. She didn't think movies lied—like many liars, she saw truth everywhere.

One day I was listening to her and I grew sad. She said angrily, "Why are you looking sad?"

I said, "Out of sympathy."

She said, "I don't want that kind of sympathy—I want to be cheered up." It was much worse, much more hysterical and shrill, than I'm showing.

"How do you want to be cheered up?"

"I don't know—you're so smart: You figure it out." But if I tried to cheer her up she'd say, "You're talking like a fool."

The Golden Rule seemed to me inadequate; she wanted something given to her that had nothing to do with what I wished for myself.

I finally caught on; she yearned for a certain kind of high-flown, movie dialogue: "Mother, is the pain *any* better today?" "No. . . . No! I can't bear it." "Didn't the nurse come today and give you the morphine shots?" I would say, sounding like a doctor, calm, fatherly. "Don't mention the morphine! I don't want to think about the morphine!" she would say like a rebellious girl or flirtatious woman.

She liked it if I pretended to be floored by her bravery whether she was being brave or not. Often she made herself up for these scenes. Lila could not bear to be just another patient for her doctors and nurses and could not bear her relative unimportance to them. My father had minded that too. But Lila plotted; she kept my report card face up on her bed when the doctor came; one day she told me to stay home from school and to cry when I let the doctor in. I said I couldn't cry. She became enraged.

It was her notion that people were good for their own pleasure or out of stupidity and were then used by people who were capable of extorting love: Love was based on physical beauty, accident, and hardness of soul; that is to say, hardness of soul aroused love in other people.

It was a perfectly good set of notions, I suppose, but I have never noticed that women thought more clearly than men.

One day I decided just to do it finally, to sit down and actually imagine myself being her, middle-aged, disfigured, and so on.

I bicycled to some woods at the edge of town—a woods cut down since—walked and carried my bicycle through the trees, until I came to a glade I knew about where there was a tiny stream between mudbanks that were in spots mossy. Enough kids used the glade that the undergrowth had been worn away in the center and the ground was mud, moist, smooth, quivering, lightly streaked with colors. As woods went, that one was threadbare, but I thought it very fine.

I'd cut my classes.

I leaned my bicycle against a tree and I sat on the moss. I'd asked Lila's sister things about what Lila was going through and the nearly senseless answers I'd gotten had unnerved me; the casual way people expressed things so that they did not tell you anything or care or ever in words admit to what they knew really bothered me. Perhaps they didn't admit it to themselves. Lila had a niece who was very intelligent and talkative but she didn't like me: It wasn't anything personal, but in the family there were assignments, and she'd been assigned to my sister; and my sister hated me, and out of politeness to my sister this cousin did not show any liking for me. She was rigorous in this (until one day she had a quarrel with my sister, and after that she was medium friendly to me). This particular cousin was outspoken and talked about things like menstruation and desiring boys, but she would not talk to me, although she was polite about not talking to me. So I didn't know if Lila was going through menopause while she was dying of cancer or not. I didn't know if one canceled the other out or not.

I don't think I made it clear to myself what I was doing. I did and I didn't know, I was definite and yet I crept up on it. Sitting in the glade, I thought it was all right and not upsetting to imagine oneself a young pretty girl, especially if you didn't do it in detail, but it seemed really foul to imagine oneself a middle-aged *woman*. It would be easiest to imagine being a very old woman, a witch, or a rude dowager—that was even sort of funny. But to think of myself as a middle-aged woman seemed to be filthy.

I wondered if I thought middle-aged women sacrosanct,

or monstrous, or disgusting, or too pathetic or what. It seemed a great transgression, a trespass to think so ill of them, although a lot of boys that I knew laughed at and scorned middle-aged women, married women and teachers both. Simply contemplating the fact, the phenomenon of middle-aged women, I seemed to myself to have entered on obscenity.

Well, then, I ought just to take them for granted and avert my eyes. But then I could not imagine what it was to be Lila or what she was going through.

All at once I did imagine myself a girl, a girl my own age; it was a flicker, a very peculiar feat—clearly I was scared to death of doing any of this. But I did it a couple of times without really pausing to experience what it was I was as a girl: I just performed the feat, I flickered into it and out again. Then, carried away by confidence, I did pause and was a girl for a second but it was so obliterating, so shocking that I couldn't stand it. I was sickened. The feeling of obliteration or castration or whatever it was was unsettling as hell.

I had more than once imagined having breasts. Other boys and I had discussed what it must be like to have breasts: We'd imitated the way girls walked; we'd put books inside our shirts to simulate the weight of breasts. But I had not imagined breasts as part of a whole physical reality. Now suddenly—almost with a kind of excitement, well, with a dry excitement as in writing out an answer to an essay question on a test, working out an outline, a structure, seeing a thing take shape—I suddenly saw how shy I'd been about the physical thing, and with what seemed to me incredible daring (and feeling unclean, coated with uncleanliness), I imagined my hips as being my shoulders: I hardly used my hips for anything; and my shoulders, which were sort of the weighty center of most of my movements and of my strength, as being my hips. I began to feel very hot; I was flushed—and humiliated. Then after a moment's thought, going almost blind with embarrassment—and sweat—I put my behind on my chest. Then I whacked my thing off quickly and I moved my hole to my crotch. I felt it would be hard to stand up, to walk, to bestir myself; I felt sheathed in embarrassment, impropriety, in transgressions that did not stay still but floated out like veils; every part of me was sexual and jutted out one way or another. I really was infinitely ashamed—there was no part of me that wasn't *dirty*, that wouldn't interfere with someone else's thoughts and suggest things. I seemed bound up, packaged, tied in this, and in extra flesh. To live required infinite shamelessness if I were like this. I was suddenly very bad-tempered. . . . (Possibly I was remembering dreams I'd had, ideas I'd had in dreams.)

I felt terrible. I tried to giggle and make it all a joke, giggle inwardly—or snort with laughter. But I felt a kind of connected hysteria, a long chain of mild hysteria, of feeling myself to be explosive, hugely important, and yet motionless, inclined to be motionless. I suddenly thought that to say no was what my pride rested on; saying yes was sloppy and killing. All this came in a rush. I was filled with impatience and incredible defiance and a kind of self-admiration I couldn't even begin to grasp. The life in me, in her, seemed a form of madness (part of me was still masculine, obviously, part of my consciousness) and maddened and mad with pleasure and also unpleasantly ashamed or stubborn. I really did feel beyond the rules, borne over the channels laid down by rules: I floated over *everything*. And there was a terrible fear-excitement thing; I was afraid-and-not-afraid; vulnerable and yet emboldened by being *dirty* and not earthbound—it was like a joke, a peculiar kind of exalted joke, a tremendous, breathless joke, one hysterical and sickening but too good for me to let go of.

I began to shake.

I had only the vaguest idea of female physical weakness —women controlled so much of the world I was familiar with, so much of University City; but all at once, almost dizzyingly, almost like a monkey, I saw—I saw *connections* everywhere, routes, methods (also things to disapprove of, and things to be enthusiastic about): I was filled with a kind of animal politics. But I was afraid of having my arms and legs broken. When I was a man, I saw only a few logical positions and routes and resting places, but as a woman I saw routes everywhere, emotional ways to get things, lies, displays of myself: It was dazzling. I saw a thousand emotional strings attached to a thousand party favors. I felt a dreadful disgust for logic—logic seemed crippling and useless, unreal; and I had the most extraordinary sense of danger—it almost made me laugh—and I had a sort of immodest pride and a kind of anguished ambition and a weird determination not to be put in danger. . . . I was filled and fascinated by a sense of myself. Physical reality was a sieve which I passed through as I willed, when my luck was good. (I had read a number of books about women: *Gone with the Wind, Pride and Prejudice, Madame Bovary.*)

Then I saw why, maybe, Lila was a terrible person—it

was her attempt at freedom. Her willfulness was all toward being free; now she was ill and caught. Briefly, I felt I understood Lila a little, only a little, for the first time. I felt I understood part of the stormy thing in her, and the thing where her pains blocked out the world and her obstinate selfishness and the feeling of having a face. I did not have entire confidence in my penetration, but still I admired my sympathy for her, but dully, almost boredly—with an open mouth, half-wondering what to think about next—when suddenly, without warning, I really imagined myself her, Lila, middle-aged, disfigured, with loose skin, my voice different from what it had been—my voice was not that of a young woman. My mouth hurt with the pressure of my bitterness: My mouth was scalded. (In my own life, when I was unhappy, it was my *eyes* that hurt; my vision would hurt me: People would look like monsters to me and would seem to have evil glances, as if black cats inhabited their eyes.) It was almost as if there were steam somewhere in my throat; really, I burned with the pressure of angry words, with a truth I wasn't willing to modify, a truth meant to be wholly destructive to the errors and selfishness of others. To their complacency. I imagined all of it—not being liked by my family any more, my husband hating me, being forsaken by my mother and sister. By my friends. As myself, as someone young, I could bear a good deal; but it takes energy to feel depressed, and when I imagined myself to be Lila, when I was Lila, I hadn't the energy any more to die; too many things had gone wrong; I was too angry to die; I felt too much; there was no end to what I felt—I could do nothing but scream.

I didn't know if I were faking all or any of this. What does imagination consist of? I was thirteen and perhaps a superficial person. There was no guarantee I felt deeply or that I possessed any human grace at all. The trees around me, the tiny creek (like an endless parade of silvery snakes of varying thinnesses rustling over pebbles), the solitude suggested to me a gravity, a decency, a balance in life that was perhaps only the reflection of my Middle Western ignorance, or idealism. It is hard to know. But as long as I held onto the power to pity her, even while I imagined myself to be her, I did not, in my deepest self, suffer what I imagined her suffering. With what I would consider the equivalent confidence and folly of a boy playing at chemistry in the basement, I held up a mental snapshot of what I had in the second before half-experienced in imagining myself to be Lila: It was a condition of mind, of terror and bitterness and hate and a trying to win out still, all churning in me, and it was evil in that it was without bounds, without any fixity or finality, and suggested an infinite nausea—I was deeply afraid of nausea. It was a condition of mind, a sickening, lightless turmoil, unbearably foul, staled; and even to imagine it without going crazy myself or bursting into tears or yelling with horror, not to live it but just to conceive of it without going through those things was somehow unclean. But with nearly infinite coldness, a coldness that was a form of love in me, I held the thought. The mind's power to penetrate these realities is not distinguishable from the mind's power merely to imagine it is penetrating reality. My father had twice contemptuously called me the Boy Scout. Did Lila live much of the time in that foulness? I thought there was no end to her wretchedness, no end—I was thirteen—to the uselessness of her misery.

The thing about being a bad person, the thing about being free and a little cheap and not letting yourself be owned by other people at all, by their emotions, was that then you had to succeed, at everything you did, all the time: Failure became an agony. And there was no alternative to that agony when it began except to become a good person. Not a saint, nothing extreme. It was just that if I imagined myself a middle-aged woman like Lila with both my breasts cut off and my husband dying, hating me while he died, turning his back on me and saying all the years he'd spent with me were foul, and with myself as selfish and hungry for triumph still, I was deprived of all justice, of all success, and my pain and terror were then so great that I would of course be insane.

Which magnified the agony.

Clearly—it seemed obvious to me as I sat there and reasoned about these things—unselfishness lessened such pain if only in the way it moved you outside your own nervous system. Generosity emptied you of any feeling of poverty anyway. I knew that from my own experience. Extended generosity predisposed you to die; death didn't seem so foul; you were already without a lot of eagerness about yourself; you were quieted.

I bicycled home, to bear the news to Momma, to tell her what I'd found out.

I was adolescent, that is I was half-formed, a sketch of a man. I told Lila unselfishness and generosity and concern for others would ease most pain, even her pain; it would make her feel better.

God, how she screamed.

She said that I came from filthy people and what I was was more filth, that I came from the scum of the earth and was more scum. Each thing she said struck her with its aptness and truth and inspired her and goaded her to greater anger. She threw an ashtray at me. She ordered me out of the house: "Sleep in the streets, sleep in the *gutter*, where you belong!" Her temper astounded me. Where did she get the strength for such temper when she was so ill? I did not fight back. My forbearance or patience or politeness or whatever it was upset her still more. I didn't catch on to this until in the middle of calling me names ("—you little bastard, you hate everybody, you're disgusting, I can't stand you, you little son of a bitch—" "Momma . . . Come on, now, Momma . . .") she screamed, "Why do you do things and make me ashamed?"

It was a revelation. It meant my *selfishness* would calm her. At first I said, "Do you really want me to go? You'll be alone here." I was partly sarcastic, laughing at her in that way, and then I began muttering, or saying with stubborn authority that I would not leave, I wanted my comfort considered, I wanted her to worry about my life. She said, huffing and gasping but less yellow and pinched and extreme, "You're a spoiled brat." I mean she was calmed to some extent; she was reduced to being incensed from being insane. But she screamed still. And I kept on too: I did not care what grounds she used—it could be on the grounds of my selfishness—but I was really stubborn: I was determined that she try being a good woman. I remember being so tense at my presumption that I kept thinking something physical in me would fail, would burst through my skin— my nerves, or my blood, my heart, everything was pounding, or my brain, but anyway that particular fight ended sort of in a draw, with Lila insulted and exhausted, appalled at what I'd said. At the stupidity. But with me adamant. I couldn't have stopped myself actually.

After that, with my shoulders hunched and my eyes on the ground or occasionally wide open and innocent for inspection and fixed on her—I referred to her always as brave and generous. I dealt with her as if she were the most generous woman imaginable, as if she had been only good to me all my life. I referred to her kindness, her bravery, her selflessness. She said I was crazy. I suppose certain accusations, certain demands, were the natural habitat of her mind. At one point she even telephoned the junior high school principal to complain I was crazy. He wouldn't listen to her. I went right on behaving as if I remembered sacrifice after sacrifice she had made for me. She was enraged, then irritated, then desperate, then bored, then nonplused, and the nonsense of it depressed her: She felt alone and misunderstood: She did not want me to be idealistic about her; she wanted me to be a companion to her, for her. But she stopped screaming at me.

I don't know if she saw through me or not. I don't think I consciously remembered over the weeks that this went on, what had started all this or its history; continued acts develop their own atmosphere; that I sincerely wanted a home of a certain kind for us was all that it seemed to be about after a while. That I had to protect myself. When she gave in, it was at first that she indulged the male of the family, the fool, the boy who was less realistic than she was. Then to conceal her defeat, she made it seem she couldn't bear to disillusion me. Also, while she more or less said that she hadn't the energy to do what I expected of her, she must have realized it took energy to fight me. She may have said to herself—as I said to myself before I imagined myself to be her—Why not? I think too my faith seduced her, my authority: I was so sure of myself. And besides, the other didn't work any more.

Of course it was a swindle all the way: She could no longer ask things of me so freely, so without thought of what it would do to me. She became resigned, and then after a while she became less sad—she even showed a wried amusement. She almost became good-tempered. She was generous to some extent with everyone or I was hurt. She reconciled with her mother and her daughter, with her brothers and her sister, with the neighbors sometimes at my insistence—even with my advice—but after a while she did it on her own in her own way. It seemed to me it was obvious that considering all the factors, she was much kinder to us than any of us were, or could be, to her, so that no matter what bargain she thought she was negotiating, she really was unselfish now. The bargain was not in her favor. She practiced a polite death or whatever, a sheltering politeness, which wasn't always phony, and a forgiveness of circumstances that was partly calculated to win friends: She comforted everyone who came near her, sometimes cornily; but still it was comfort. I was a little awed by her; she was maybe awed and instructed by herself; she took over the—the *role*—and my opinions were something she asked, but she had her own life. Her own predicament. She still denounced people behind their backs but briefly, and she gloated now and then: When her rich brother died suddenly, she said with a gently melancholy satisfaction, "Who would have thought I could outlast J.J.?" She showed a shakily calm and remarkable daily courage; she made herself, although she was a dying woman, into a woman who was good company. She put together a whole new set of friends. Those friends loved her actually, they looked up to her, they admired her. She often boasted, "I have many, many very good friends who have stuck by me." But they were all new friends—none of her old friends came back. Young people always liked her now and envied me. What was so moving was her dying woman's gaiety—it was so unexpected and so unforced, a kind of amusement with things. Sometimes when no one was around she would yell at me that she was in pain all the time and that I was a fool to believe the act she put on. But after a certain point, that stopped too. She said, "I want to be an encouragement—I want you to remember me as someone who was a help to you." Do you see? After a certain time she was never again hysterical when I was there. Never. She was setting me an example. She was good to me in a way possible to her, the way she thought she, Lila, ought to be to me. But she was always Lila, no matter how kind she was. If at any time restlessness showed in me or if I was unhappy even about something very minor at school she would be upset; I had to have no feelings at all or stay within a narrow range for her comfort; she said often, "I know I'm unfair but wait until I die—can't you bear with me?" When I stayed out sometimes because I had to, because I was going crazy, when I came home she would say pleadingly, "Don't ask too much of me, Wiley." She would sit there, on the couch in the living room, having waited fully dressed for me to come home, and she would say that.

All right, her happiness rested on me. Her sister and one brother and her daughter told me I couldn't go to college, I couldn't leave Lila, it would be a crime. Her cancer was in remission; she had never gotten on so well with her own family (she was patient with them now), I owed it to her to stay. I am trying to establish what she gained and what she lost. Her family often said to me bullyingly, without affection, or admiration, "Her life is in your hands." I hadn't intended this. Lila said they were jealous of me. I wanted to go to college; I wanted to use my mind and all that: I was willing for Lila's life to be in her mother's and sister's hands. I was modest about what I meant to Lila—does that mean I didn't love her?

The high school, when I refused to apply to Harvard, asked me why and then someone went to see Lila, and Lila went into her bedroom and locked the door and refused to eat until I agreed to go away to college. To leave her. And she made her family and her doctor ask me to go (they pounded on her door but she wouldn't eat until they did what she told them). Lila's sister Beth came and shouted through the bedroom door at her and then said to me in a cutting, angry voice, blaming me, that Lila was killing herself. This was when I was sixteen.

I said I wasn't that important. My modesty stymied Beth.

That sacrifice, if it was that, was either the first or second thing Lila had ever done for me. But perhaps she did it for herself, to strengthen her hand for some Last Judgment. Perhaps she was glad to be rid of me. I lost my nerve only once, in accepting it from her, this gift. I was lying on my bed—it was evening in early spring and I should have been doing Physics—and I was thinking about college, Harvard, about a place, the Yard, that I'd never seen, grass and paths and a wall around it, and buildings and trees, an enclosed park for young people. The thought took me to a pitch of anticipation and longing and readiness unlike anything I'd felt in years; all at once it was unendurable that I had that and Lila had nothing—had what she had. It was terrible to think how Lila was cheated in terms of what she could see ahead of her. I felt I'd tricked her in some way. Not that that was wrong but she was too nice, now that she was cheated, for me to—I don't know what. I suppose I was out of control. Clumsy, even lumbering, I blundered into her room and without warning or explanation began to say I was sorry and that I'd better back out of going to Harvard. She breathed in the loud, nervous way of a woman concerned about herself, but then she got herself in hand and said in the detached, slightly ironic voice, gentle, convivial, and conspiratorial that she used at that time, a Middle Western voice, "Sorry for what? What is it? Wiley, you have nothing to be sorry for."

I'd never brought up in conversation with her matters that had to do with feelings of mine that were unclear or difficult: What good would it have done? She would not have made the effort to understand; she did not know how; she would only have felt lousy and been upset. I was silenced by a long tradition of lying to her and being lucid. I could at this time only say over and over that I was sorry—

I couldn't try to explain any of it to her.

She said, "You're being silly. I think you're too close to me, Wiley. I don't want you to grow up to be a mother's boy."

I said, "What will you do when I go away?"

"You think I can't manage? You don't know much about me. Don't be so conceited where you're concerned." (But I'd put that idea into the air.) She said, "I can manage very well, believe me." I expressed disbelief by the way I stared at her. She said, "Go into my top bureau drawer. Look under the handkerchiefs."

There was a bottle there. I held it up. "What is it?"

"My morphine."

"You hide it?"

"I know how boys like to try things . . ."

"You hide it from *me?*"

"I don't want you to be tempted—I know you're often under a strain."

"Momma, I wouldn't take your *morphine.*"

"But I don't use it much any more. Haven't you noticed I'm clearer lately? I don't let myself use it, Wiley—look at the date on the bottle: It's lasted over a year. The doctor can't believe I'm so reformed; he'll ask me to marry him yet. Just sometimes I take it on a rainy day. Or at night. I thought you knew I wasn't using morphine any more."

I hadn't noticed. I hadn't been keeping track. I didn't like to be too aware of her.

She could have had another bottle hidden; there was a nurse who came twice a week and who could, and I think did, give Lila injections of morphine. I didn't want to investigate. Or know. I just wanted to go on experiencing the release of having her care about me. Worry about me. She said, "You've been a help to me. You've done more than your share. You know what they say—out of the mouths of babes. I'll be honest with you: I'd like to be young again, I'd like to have my health back. But I'm not unhappy. I even think I'm happy now. Believe me, Wiley, the pain is less for me than it was."

At Harvard, I began to forget her. But at times I felt arrogant because of what she and I had done; I'd managed to do more than many of my professors could. I'd done more than many of them would try. I knew more than they did about some things.

Often I felt I was guilty of possessing an overspecialized maturity. At times I felt called upon to defend Lila by believing the great world to which Harvard was a kind of crooked door was worthless in its cruelty and its misuse of its inhabitants and Lila was more important than any of it. Than what I had come to Harvard for. But I didn't go home.

And Lila wanted me to enter that great world: The only parts of my letters she really enjoyed were about things like my meeting a girl whose mother was a billionairess. By the standards of this new world I was sentimental and easily gulled and Lila was shrill. I did not want to see beyond a present folly or escape from one or be corrected or remember anything. Otherwise, the shadow of Lila lay everywhere. I began to forget her even while she was alive.

The daughter of the billionairess was, in addition to

everything else, a really admirable and intelligent girl. But I didn't trust her. One night she confessed various approaches she followed for winning the affection of boys. If you don't want to be silly and overly frail, you have to be immune and heartless to the fine-drawn, drawn-out, infinitely ludicrous, workable plots that women engage in. The delicacy and density of those plots. But I wasn't confident and I ran away from that girl. It seemed to me my whole life was sad. It was very hard to bear to see that in the worldly frame of Harvard Lila was, even in her relative nobility, unimportant. I had never been conscious before of the limitations of her intelligence. She had asked me to send her money and I did, my freshman year. I had a scholarship and I worked. It wasn't any longer that she was jealous of my life but she wanted me to show I cared about her still. She had changed her manner just before I left her; she had become like a German-Jewish matron of the sort who has a son at Harvard. And her letters were foolish, almost illiterate. It was too much for me, the costliness of loyalty, the pursuit of meanings, and everything savage from the past, half-forgotten or summarized (and unreal) or lost in memory already. How beautiful I thought the ordinary was. I did not go home to live with her and she did not ask me to, when, after three years of remission, and three months after my leaving her, her cancer recurred.

How can I even guess at what she gained, what she lost?

I spent the summer with her. I had a job and stayed home with her in the evenings. My manner unnerved her a bit. I was as agreeable as I knew how to be; I tried to be as Middle Western as before. When company came, Lila would ask me to stay only for a little while and then to excuse myself and leave: "People pay too much attention to you, and I like a little attention for myself."

The Christmas after that, I traveled out to be with her, fell ill and was in a delirium for most of two weeks. Lila was curiously patient, not reproachful that I'd been ill, not worried, and when we spoke it was with a curious peace, and caution too, as if we were the only two adults in the world. She said for the first time, "I love you, Wiley."

In May I was called to her bedside because she was about to die. Her family had gathered and they stood aside, or else Lila had told them to leave us alone; perhaps they recognized my prior right to her; they had never been able to get along with her, they had only loved her. Lila said, "I was waiting for you. It's awful. Mose comes in here and complains about his health and carries on about me and doesn't hear me ask for water, and Beth cries and says it's terrible for her, Beth was never any good at a deathbed—and your sister comes in here and says, 'Have a little nap,' and when I close my eyes she runs to the dresser and looks at things: She's afraid I left it all to you; she already took my compact and she uses it in front of me. I wasn't a good mother but she doesn't have to rub it in. She thinks I'm dead already. Her feelings are hurt. How is college? What I'd like to hear about is the rich people you've met. . . ."

When I started to speak, she cut in: "I was afraid you

wouldn't get here in time. I didn't want to interrupt your studies and I was afraid I waited too long. I didn't let them give me a morphine shot today. I want to talk to you with a clear head. The pain is not good, Wiley, but I don't want to be drugged when we talk. I've been thinking what I would say to you. I've been thinking about it all week. I like talking to you. Listen, I want to say this first: I appreciate what you did for me, Wiley."

"I didn't do anything special for you." I did not remember clearly—I had put it out of my mind . . . I did not want any responsibility for Lila.

"Wiley, you were good to me," she said.

"Well, Momma, you were good to *me*." I was too shy, too collegiate, too anxious to praise her, too rattled by the emergency, by the thought she was dying to say anything else. I thought it would be best for us to go on to the end, as we had gone on for so long. For so many years I'd calmed and guided her this way: It was an old device. I assumed I couldn't be honest with her now. I had no notion that dying had educated her. I was eighteen, a young man who had a number of voices, who was subject to his own angers, to a sense of isolation that made him unwilling to use his gifts. In Cambridge, people I knew applied adjectives to me in the melodramatic way of college sophomores: interesting, immature, bad-tempered. There were people who were in love with me. I was intensely unhappy and knew a great deal of it I owed to Lila.

Lila said, "I've been waiting for you. I missed you, Wiley. Listen, I'm not as strong as I was. I can't put on too good a show—if I make faces or noises, don't get upset and run for the nurse: Let me talk: You make things too easy for me. Now listen, don't get mad at me but you have to promise me you'll finish college—you tend to run away from things. You're lazy, Wiley. Promise me: I have to make you promise—I want to be a good mother—will wonders never cease?"

"You always were a good mother."

"Oh, Wiley, I was terrible."

"No, Momma. No, you weren't." But I think she wanted companionship, not consolation; I guessed wrong on that last occasion. She said, "We don't have to be polite to each other now—Wiley, will you say you forgive me?"

She thought I was happy and strong, that I'd survived my childhood. I wanted her to think that. So far as I knew I didn't blame her, not for anything; but not-blaming someone is very unlike forgiving them: If I were to forgive her it meant I had first to remember. I would have collapsed sobbing on her bed and cried out, God, it was so awful, so awful, why did those things have to happen, oh God, it was so awful. . . .

I don't know if I was cruel or not. I told her I wasn't being polite, that I had nothing to forgive her for: "You were a good mother."

She said, "Wiley, you helped me—I can bear the pain."

"Momma!" I refused to understand. "You did it all yourself. You were always better than you thought."

Each breath she took was like a seesaw noisily grinding aloft, descending. Her life was held in a saucer on that seesaw. I have no gift for bearing human pain. I kept thinking, I can accept this, I can do this without getting hysterical.

"It was always easier for me than you thought, Mother; you never hurt me much; you always thought you were worse than you were. A lot of what you blame yourself for was always imaginary—you were better to me than anyone else was—at least, you lived."

"Wiley, I can face the truth, I know what I did."

"I don't know what you did."

And she even forgave me that. She said, "I understand. You don't want to face things now. Maybe it's better not to bring it up."

"Do what you like, Momma. I'll understand sooner or later."

She said, "Kiss me, Wiley. Am I very ugly?"

"No, Momma."

"You always thought I was pretty. Listen, at the end, Wiley, I tried. I loved you. I'm ready to die, I'm only alive because I wanted to talk to you, I wanted that to be the last thing—do you understand, I want you to know now how much I think of you."

"Momma—"

"I'm going to die soon, I'm very bad, Wiley. Listen: I don't want you to grieve for me. You've done your share already. I want you to have a good time. I want you to enjoy yourself." Then she said, "I can't be what you want; I don't want to upset you; just say you forgive me."

"I will if you give me your forgiveness, Momma."

"My forgiveness? Oh Wiley. I bet you're good with girls. What a liar you are. And I always thought I was a liar. I forgive you, Wiley. Don't you know what you did for me? You made it so the pain was less."

"Momma, I didn't do anything."

"Isn't it funny what people are ashamed of?" She was silent for a small second; then she said, "Do you forgive me?"

"I forgive you, Momma, but there's nothing to forgive you for. If it wasn't for you I'd be dead."

"That was a long time ago, you were still a baby then. Oh. Run now and get the nurse. I don't think I can stand the pain now. Tell her I want my shot."

After the nurse had gone, Lila said, "Wiley, I went in a wheelchair to the ward where people had cancer and were frightened, and I tried to help them—I thought you would be proud of me."

For a moment, I remembered something. *"Momma, I was a stupid boy."*

"Hold my hand while I fall asleep, Wiley. I don't know I think Harvard is such a good place—you don't face things as well as you used to. Wiley, I'm tired of it all. I don't like my family much. Is it terrible to say I don't think they're nice people? In the end you and my father were the only ones. I wish you could have known him. I loved you best. Don't let it go to your head. You never thought you were conceited but you were—that's always the part of the story you leave out—and how you like to domineer over people. It's a miracle no one's killed you yet. It's terrible to be sorry for things. Wiley, do you know why that is, why is it terrible to be sorry? I don't know why things happened the way they did. I kept thinking as I lay here it would be interesting if I understood things now and I could tell you —I know how you like to know things. Wiley, I promised your mother you would remember her—promise me you'll think well of her. She was your real mother and she loved you too. Wiley?"

"Yes."

"Find someone to love. Find someone to be good to

you." Then she said, "I love you, Wiley. . . . I'm sorry."

She seemed to sleep. Then her breathing grew rough. I thought I ought to go get the doctor but then I sat down again and stared at the ceiling. I was afraid my feeling for her or some flow of regret in me or anything in me she might as a woman feel as a thread requiring her attention would interfere with her death. So I said to myself, You can die, Momma; it's all right; I don't want you to live any more. From time to time, in her sleep, in her dying, she shouted, "Haven't I suffered enough?" and "Wiley, are you still there? Don't have anything to do with those terrible people!" Then she came to and said, "Am I shouting things? . . . I thought so. I don't want you to go away but when you're this close I don't feel right."

"Do you want me to go into the hall?"

"No. Don't leave me. But don't sit too close to me, don't look at me. Just stay near. . . . I want you here."

"All right, Momma."

I listened to her breathing grow irregular. I said to myself, Die, Momma. On this breath. I don't want you to live any more. Her breath changed again. It began to be very loud, rackety. I began to count her breaths. I counted fifteen and then neither her breath nor her actual voice was ever heard again.

After she died, I had a nervous breakdown. I couldn't believe I missed her that much. I'd loved her at the end, loved her again, loved and admired her, loved her greatly; of course, by that time, she did not ask that the love I felt express itself in sacrificing myself for her. I loved her while I enjoyed an increasing freedom from her but still I needed her; and, as I said, I had a nervous breakdown when she died. After a while, I got over it.

I don't know all that I gained or lost, either. I know I was never to be certain I was masculine to the proper degree again. I always thought I knew what women felt.

Make what use of this you like.

ANGEL

✒ Today The Angel of Silence and of Inspiration (toward Truth) appeared to a number of us passing by on the walk in front of Harvard Hall—this was a little after three o'clock—today is October twenty-fifth, nineteen-hundred-and-fifty-one.

The shadow came first. In my case, I looked up to see if the sky had clouded over and saw instead with amazing shock the rudiments of a large face, not in any perspective, but a face-like thing that was also a figure, not with feet nearest me, then legs and so on, and not frontal but smoothly and yet crudely present in all the visual and mental ways figures and faces sometimes are for me in my dreams.

It was like the shifting sense of things in dreams, seen and known in varied ways; and what was paramount was an observing—and kind but not forward—*facedness*, a prow of knowing making Itself known—A Countenance, not human, not exactly—or entirely—inhuman, conceivably human in relation, but one that did not suggest It ever knew unconsciousness or error—or slyness—and I was startled but not made insane but was student-like—but not at once awed into complete readiness to be changed in every part of myself, but that came within seconds, as the world, the visible bricks and roofs, trees, leaves, people, lost color and shrank in scale—by comparison.

It has been cider-like weather; and local faces are not yet as badly strained as they will be in a few weeks in the shorter days and the realities of study and competition here (Harvard). The crypt-and-ghost pallors of ambition and mental hubris have hatched some of our moth-like look, we devourers of stored fabrics of emotion, but only a few of us are exemplars of whiteness—that is to say, faces have flecks of leftover health but it's a more and more remote pink they have, the complexion of a fire in a veil—fire dressed as a bride for an unknown groom—and The New Figure was white indeed, but the white of all the colors, as if it were dressed in prisms.

People are somewhat gorgeous collections of chemical fires, aren't they? Cells and organs burn and smoulder, each one, and hot electricity flows and creates storms of further currents, magnetisms and species of gravity—we are towers of kinds of fires, down to the tiniest constituents of ourselves, whatever those are, those things burn like stars in space, in helpless mimicry of the vastness out there, electrons and neutrons, planets and suns, so that we are made of universes of fires contained in skin and placed in turn within a turning and lumbering universe of fires through which This Figure had clearly traveled and about which It knew, one assumed, or felt, and on which It was an improvement, being unchemical, unthought, decidedly unitary as if Its fires were not widely scattered as all others were, as if It were a steady and unparticled fire, or as if It were invulnerable (by human measure) and white and yet with colors and without fire at all.

At any rate, a whiteness spread, and everything and everyone is chalk and blackboard, and is will and grammar like dried and leafless branches of the trees in the dire light of a December but at the same time, it was a scouring bliss. The sloppy Armaggedons of fucking with girls comes to mind; the air is damp and chill and pale and white, a celebratedly dead light for Puritans, not a punishing light, but perhaps a fools' light, cold, pale, and as if spitefully luminous; and then it grows dry—and relentless—but it remains a dead light.

I don't mean to be paradoxical but I thought of The Creature of Light at that time as The Shadow I guess because It had been cast by A Brighter Light—It was A Mechanism or Device, It was not a living thing as we, the watchers, were.

The Shadow seemed to touch and take the attention of perhaps half a hundred people, a random Cambridge mélange of men and women, some few children, students, an uninteresting sample of the ambitious and troubled American privileged, and then the world beyond—i.e., Cambridge—was banished and went about its business unilluminated, although at the time it was not known if the rest of the world had been destroyed or not.

One was as if inside a dreaming skull. The Figure had no Great Light or Clarity at first or Clear Dimension or Knowable Perspective except that it seemed in a logically apparent way to be somewhat taller than Harvard Hall.

The altered light named itself at once in exclamatory

thought and in strange confusion of soul, *A Doomsday Light*; I am in my willful identification of myself, Jewish; but perhaps my Jewishness has long since rotted away except as a root—I have often been so accused—but even so, my Jewishness is also the absence of Pagan weight and detail and gloom and of Christian secular frivolity and sacred populism: I was often enough accused of that in college.

But I am not Christian. I do not feel in my soul any right or privilege of immediate access to the Divine, the Divine that once took *human* form and suffered excruciatingly as we do. Nor do I think prayer is answered by Figures who just as a man being hanged or a woman in childbirth or being fucked is so entirely available to our usages of eyes and thoughts and physical action if we so desire, if we are not prevented, so was Divinity on the cross and is still as Suffering Mother or Father or Son or Wisdom. That Divinity in such a form causes, in one's thoughts, a curious mingling of impious and pious etiquettes, presumptions and pride, charities and pieties, an entire texture of horror and justices and permissions which is present because of these beliefs and only these, and because no other conceivable actuality could supply authority for that Christian texture I think of as *Christian*—I am excluded from that although not entirely: I am a borderline figure, renegade or climber—or herald. It is not so far known about me what I am—history and life have not decided yet.

I was Christian enough to expect to see further Figures, many with trumpets and swords, rising in spirals upward or arranged in tiers ascending toward the soon-to-be-revealed Ultimate Radiance, God the Father, and I felt this, I confess, as a Jewish defeat—but since I thought it was, indeed, The End of the World, that querulous home team rooting silenced itself in expectation of justice, logic, orderliness of a divine sort at last.

I was born and had so far lived among those who considered it a life's work to fight that creeping urgency—of Apocalypse—that final tantrum of would-be and assuredly horrible Explanation and Meaning, but now I found in myself a Fascist or willful or demonically proud element that welcomed it—half-welcomed it, to be honest.

No wholesale hosannahs broke from me—or the others there—outwardly or resounded in my soul inwardly except as a kind of test to see how it felt to think that.

But that's not true either quite, and some hosannahs did resound in me and in odd tonalities—and, as I implied, some were, maybe most were, made up of inner whispers and doubts.

Clearly, a great variety of doctrines and secret beliefs were present among the watchers, and I found I was aware of that—that I was aware of more than The Angel and of more than myself—and that under the pressure of meanings and of possibilities now, and of verification—or *proof* —as some people present took it—many people present fainted but remained erect—only a few fell; and some shouted or started to; others turned their backs to the manifestation as if incurious (in order to protect a seated faith) of those in that posture, some then cried out; some waited or peered; some were doubtingly curious and adopted postures of supplication—the women present were more fainthearted—i.e., less trusting, more careful—the men were more overcome with Christian dread in one form or another

and with Jewish exaltation and pride and readiness to celebrate or with Jewish fear and resignation, or so I read their
postures, that and now the words on paper, these words, in
part breed themselves from unnoticed information earlier
and in unlit parts of my mind according to odd effects they
have on each other as utterance, once the utterance is made.

And, in this case, I find the extreme conceit of speech to
be shattering.

The Catholics were the most startled—the people I assumed were Catholics, promptly the palest—or whitest—
ones, with dark circles around their eyes and a look of
knowledge, confession and surrender and The Idea of Hell.

Whitely, like poor mirrors of The Seraph, in oddly an-
gled postures, often leaning back and with one or both arms
raised, we mostly stared directly toward The Face of the
Seraphic Messenger—all of whom, light and imputed arms
and seeming feet, was face—and most of those who cried
out did so wanly, and many were not conscious for much of
the time at first although they stood upright, to some extent: Very few people kneeled, or remained kneeling—
there was a lot of stillness of response but there was no
stillness of response at all, if you see what I mean—some
people stared down at the ground, and only a few faces
showed any trust at all, any real obedience of soul: that
steely masochism that requires so much training. We merely
looked, we partially looked, at It, someone kneeled slowly
at a certain moment, and many others, prompted, slowly
did so, too; and then they rose again mostly, but some did
not, among the trees, in That White, Dead Light.

I confess I felt mostly shock and doubt; I was blinkingly,
rebelliously, impiously, ineptly disrespectful and restless

among moments of severe awe, even at first; I was withdrawn, then attentive, then withdrawn again differently: My attention, my attentiveness, my strained and straining openness, my aching openness, the struggle to be open with no self-defense was not single-hearted—I resisted The Announcement, The Inspiration, The Angel, The Seraphic Messenger, not that I doubted that the soul (which is, in a way, the whole of what we have done in the light of what has been done to us) in its distances of belief—philosophy and awe—was not at bottom *childlike-and-pious* but could ignore the child in me to some extent even when, if I may be permitted to say this, God in this form faced me.

The Great Seraph did not seem to be, in any sense, *militant*—not the least *military*—or, for that matter, musical either. It was neither distant nor fond, It was not commanding or alluring; the phenomenon of Itself was of rare abilities on a not-human base—but related—compacted here into a somewhat recognizable Figure—somewhat recognizable—considerably larger than I was, more undeniably fine than anything I had ever seen, more conscious, but oddly in a way, so that I do not know and I did not know then, I did not know and I had no continuous faith, no conviction about what It was conscious of—love, say, or distant patience, or what. I was aware even then that others saw It differently—as Patience, say, or as Love, or as Militance—but to me It signified nothing, not even the degree to which It was willful and what It might or might not do or say—It only represented Beauty and Meaning, which is to say Truth, but not my truth so far, which is to say, then, New Truth—ungraspable at first—and perhaps always—and It was partly Old Truth from which I had strayed—but Truth would always be so new, as new as This Figure was, that one might then be slightly—or even strongly—driven to slighting behavior toward It as a result.

Impiety. Self-defense. Rebellion. Whatever.

Those were clearer to me—those modes of resistance—than was the terror of what Acceptance would bring.

It seems to me now it was impiety or selfishness on my part to think that except as the end of things It was not otherwise humanly relevant. It was relevant at its own say-so.

I noticed that It seemed to be overwhelmingly *suitable*—I wanted suddenly to be like It; this struck me at the second I felt it, this desire as it formed, that it was now the supreme fact of my life, this esthetic, this being influenced by a function of the Angel's quality—this was *Love*, I presume, for an apparition, one that affected my senses, a reality, an appearance.

The absence of vengeance in Its stance and Its being without any of the accoutrements of myth—It carried no symbols, It was dressed in nothing but undefinability, It was not dressed or undressed, It was not naked, It was neutrally and luminously clear and unclear—It was contentedly beyond the need of further signification—It would never be modified or added to, argued with, corrected, or moved—that is, It was post-Apocalyptic: I fell in love with It as *The End and Be-All*, I fell in love with silence—Its silence anyway.

But the mind, bemused or sanctified or not, in love and a-soar and wishing to be obedient, does not cease to feel and wobble—wobble means think—it discards thoughts and feelings as they draw notice, as they appear they are dismissed: But still one's heart vibrates, too, between attention and inattention or rather, between low desire—physical desire—and a wish *consciously* (i.e., sinlessly) to know—without physical will—but one gives in to physical desire anyway as feeling if not as act: I did not walk toward The Angel—not more than a few feet, if that; perhaps I imagined it. I expired in a kind of light. The Angel was suitable and I was not but I imagined an embrace, my will having its way with this Lighted *suitability* that had altered history and was altering it now, without apparently being altered by any of this. *My God, my God.* I thought The Angel had ended history. I thought I ought to walk in The White Furnace of Its Glory—The Grand Wars of God, The Chambers of Holocaust—Daniel and Joseph—I don't know what my ego and heart and soul were thinking of—It was there, The Angel, and merely in Its being present, It made it stupid to lie; and this was so whether It was an Angel or a hoax, or rather, It could not be a useless hoax since It was authentically, irregularly, idiosyncratically joy and awe and so summoning and wonderful in Its form. I longed to know how the others there felt This Apparition, but it seemed pointless finally since our opinions did not matter, and since so long as It was present, we were not commanded by ourselves, by our opinions, or by each other but only by It, Its presence. It hadn't occurred to me before this moment that ours was a species of habitual judgment, but now that this faculty of conscious mind was useless—assent and praise were hardly required—I did think, with some unclarity, that Judgment Day like now would be an occasion of the banishing of judgment from us. This seemed tremendously sexual. It was awful to know my life had to change beyond my power to influence or judge or analyze or find Reason—I could not limit the new consciousness except by unconsciousness, by fainting. Mind would change in the light of Possibility inherent in the fact of The Seen Angel—Its Goodness, Its Forbearance: It did NO HUMAN THING. We saw This Angel and It did nothing, This Particular One, Its Appearance, It was one Angel and not an *example* of anything—it could not be multiplied or divided —by us, by our minds, by mine. It was *A Thing*, a kind of Silent Goodness, but not an example. Governed by Revelation in this form is a tremendous thing and unmanning much as when a woman says, *All right, I will tell you a truth or two,* and she means it as an act of rule, and what she then says, does affect you, if it does, if the revelation changes the way you think, it does make you crazed and weak, perhaps: You are in an unknown place or facet of consciousness: It was like this but much, much, much more so. It was at this point that I went down on my knees and then, after a second, rose again, choosing to stand in the face of This Androgynous Power, which being of this order of magnitude and of this maternal a quality yet seemed male to me.

Of course, It was perceived by others according to different bodies of symbols derived from their lives and dreams —and they saw It as warlike or virgin-maidenly—or virgin-maidenly-and-warlike or as like a father and not at all in the way that I saw It. For some, It was Pure Voice and Radiance and not a figure at all—but for everyone I spoke to or looked at, It was Actuality—and It could be ignored or interpreted as one liked but only at one's peril—that was admitted.

It was glumly radiant inside a spreading bell of altered light, not the light of a dream, the light of thought. Perhaps the light of unquestioned and unbelievably Correct Thought of a sort no one has yet had, a thought so Correct, I cannot imagine It transmitted to me without my becoming capable of holding It, i.e., equal to It, similar to It—husband or wife to It. It was what my teachers and lovers and acquaintances claimed to possess in their arguments, an undeniable Truth, visible to all—within the radius of Its light. To have comprehended It would have made me an angel roughly to the extent It was one—just as scholars, at colleges especially, feel they have mastered and by mastering, have surpassed (and brought up to date) the men and women whose work they interpret. Humility is a very difficult state in its reality, difficult to maintain. The statement or claim, the profession of it is easy enough. But the Angel was not like Christ or anything human in terms of vulnerability—It was not equal in any sense—It did not mitigate Its authority for an instant. An unchosen humility is very peculiar—it oozes through the self and distorts the framework of one's identity—the foundation of the self is pride. But pride was gone —off and on—in the presence of The Angel—it was Very Sexual, as I said. I would think that love must abandon any sort of hope of a limit to the finality of caring, no limit exists to that ruthlessness except in the will to disobey. Final rightness would explode you—The Angel's was not final. If the truth is not final, then it is not greater than me beyond all endurance—The Angel did not end my life. A belief that permits questions is human. Any entirely true belief ends any problem of will. I did not believe The Angel was of that manner of authority after the first few seconds

—perhaps a minute all told. The light of The Angel lay among trees which had individual leaves and clusters of leaves in a familiar and regular scale but diminished in the fraught depths of their real dimensions in Its presence in the powerful and upsetting light, the unspeakably peculiar but very beautiful radiance of the eerie Seraph.

To survive—as in my dreams when I am threatened with death—it is not believable that one will live, and one doesn't live longer in the dream; one wakes to cynicism, to morning air, to faith of a sort.

But the nearby buildings and paths and faces were not dream-like. The sky beyond The Shadow and The Figure was real sky. Nothing became less real in that light, merely less important *for the moment*. It became less interesting than the light itself, than what stood so tall-y and so change-able and stilly at the center of the light—time had stopped for It to some degree, although my breath and my heart-beat continued—that stood so forbearingly and goadingly and silently. . . .

This manifestation of meaning and silence—it was comic to think—overrode several fields of study, lives' work, no-tions of guilt and convictions of sins and sinlessness, and most theories so far, a great many things all in all—but not everyone present perceived It as The Angel of Silence. Many thought It spoke but no two agreed about the speech they claimed for It. As usual, the visions of audible or writ-ten or seen grace were solitary—except The Angel was present to a number of us, all who were there, who were not clever or devious. Everything was changed, was under-cut. Being a student and largely without family and not solidly in love although I loved a few people, a foolish selection as usual, I was susceptible, I was ready, for the obliteration of Old Thought in this anxious excitement, as suffocating as an asthma, of The Angel's Silent Truth, Its Testimony by means of presence and silence—undoubted presence individually, doubtful only socially although everyone within the bell of light agreed Something Extraordinary had been present—unless they thought it clever to hedge, to pretend to a more complex sense of human politics afterward than the rest of us. Extraordinary—and of extraordinary merit to us, to me.

That is too mild but I am trying to avoid error. I admitted It was an Angel. If It was fake, It was impressive enough to convert me to what It stood for, although I didn't know what that was, yet, but I would spend my life searching, perhaps not monomaniacally but with considerable persistence for Its Meaning. The readiness for this in me, the credulity if you like, submissive and sportive, violent and pacifistic and partly rebellious in turn, became my irreverence which burned like a titanic shame—a terrible and yet naïve and entire *amusement*, perhaps lifelong. It hardly seemed a matter of spirit and belief in a fancy way so much as a kind of anecdotal thing about me being dragged into the proximity of Holiness—and Holy Vision—now seen as a vast suitability beyond my powers of judgment and not requiring my assent in any form. Holiness manifested Itself, remained silent, and excluded me, mind and spirit and body—but not my emotions—and included me in a certainty of knowledge about Something for which The Creature of Light was an emissary but of which I could hardly speak.

It was not perverse or wrong—it was *suitable*—appropriate—*I* was perverse and wrong.

The direction of The Hinted Doctrine and of the change overall that was called for by the sight of The Figure was just not clear. Human inventions, human crimes were not descried. Nor did The Angel seem to be any sort of absolute example of anything—even of eternity. The awe I felt at the beginning of The Manifestation had within itself that startling power of truth of a film of a seedling growing over a period of months; the film is continuous; then the film is edited and shows the seedling forcing its way through pavements and into an as-if-eternal sun, and the film is true although one will never see such a thing as it shows.

Some of the *truth* I felt as present, some of the meaning was false such as that it, my awe, would soon not be parenthetical but be worldwide, then universal, then eternal, more than a world conquest, a conquest of space and Time, but this was not the case. I was *passively* evangelical, expectantly evangelical—which is perhaps a middle-class cast of soul—but nothing happened of that sort.

I was not sad. My expectation of eternity, my sense of Revelation here, contains, in a startling form, my belief, hidden to me until this moment (when Eternity or something partway to It showed Itself but did not adopt me and take me within Itself) of a common and individually willed but universal disrespect in us—because the power—love or force—was never in fact absolute—irresistible—final. I don't know why so absolute an object—which would crush me— was desirable—or perhaps it wasn't; perhaps it's just that one knows one would have to love absolute power absolutely—the soul has odd twists and knowledges of politics in it. Deity, in the form of some reasonably final force, was showing Itself, was showing It did not mean to bridle this time either the disobedient and spiritually incoherent species. No finality—such as the rising up of the dead—occurred to make this clearly the ultimate moment. Disrespect and its inevitable companion, sentimentality, were then at once as apparent in us—(me)—as the silence of The Apparition was an aspect of It—if you compared stories.

A great many people present must have wanted to deny It as I did not. Disrespectful—and sentimental—as I was, I was willing to accede to It (even if It was an error, a hoax) from the start, partly I think because It was not dressed in gold but mostly because It was so lovely in the way It was *suitable*; but I'm a sort of orphan; and others must have wanted to preserve their investments and truths, partial truths and nervous lies and disrespect, as not symbols but Truths. They did not want to de-fuse the power of lies to obliterate the powers of the mind—I must say I was uneasy and sickened by it—the thought of truth, Truth, TRUTH, TRUTH. The deep sense of value they had in their lives made them seek some emotional or sexual message that would leave them intact, that would be the rest of their inheritance, so to speak; whereas I knew you would have to throw yourself away entirely—entirely—if you wanted to come to being able to bear TRUTH—of course, then you wouldn't know ordinary truth, the truth of most people, and, so, you couldn't speak either; you'd have to make your way back, so to speak: It was in the myths and metaphors, I'd read about it, I'd dreamed about it. To respect this has never been hard for me but it was sickening to start to live it through: and there was no ceremony of denial or of mutual agreement, no asking if you wanted to see This, no testing of the reality of the affection of The Apparition, no formal establishment of ceremony concerning The Somewhat Final Dignity of The Actuality of The Seraph and making It bearable—or whatever.

It did not speak. It spared us. I can theorize about *Holy Speech*, the Timeless rending Itself to make one syllable of somewhat businesslike utterance—one syllable would be all It would have to say if It chose to speak at all and not simply occupy everyone's mind and all matter—more easily than I can about the possible speech of The Actual Angel. It would have stammered, It would have been loud, It would have been sky-y trumpets and an earthquake, a known language, a mixture of lion's pure vastness of temper and self-will and a mother's exhausted or defiantly unworn lullaby. Listening to it would have been one of those epic affairs of *Listen, comprehend very fast, comprehend at once, or die or nearly die,* as in childhood, or as when one is in love, or, when as in first grade, one must learn to read in order not to doom oneself in relation to The Middle Class and money and Ordinary Thought; or as in a fist fight or as in a battle. One is very attentive in those cases. It is hard, nonetheless, to make out the sense of what is happening. One tries, and the moment takes on a transcendence from that trial, if one does succeed at all at the grace of listening. By which I mean The Angel could have trained us or could simply have implanted knowledge in us and not be bothered with words if It chose. But The Angel was silent even in that sense as if It was too democratically inclined, Its knowledge of justice was too great for It to consider such coercion.

It never did speak but in the actual moment it was very strange not to know or to be able to guess what It would say when It should speak soon as one expected It would. I had once or twice in my childhood thought about, noted, even imagined tones in The Tactful Silence of Deity— imagined tempting and taunting It, or earning from It an omen or sign. I had once held an idea that an Angel need not and might not speak. But in the moment, I was afraid and I hoped for the trial of attempting to grasp Its Word and in being judged consequently. In the weight of the truth of Its Appearance, in the presence of the marvelous, one would struggle vastly, terribly, when a Seraph spoke, homosexually, I would think, to be a True Ear and to understand and respond faithfully, to show docility. One would be like a child again, immortally, irrevocably vulnerable, one would hope to be the favored son, the soul most blessed by Divinity as shown in one's comprehension, one's response and perception of the penetration of the message, of the occasion of Angelic speech. I say this from deduction. I see how Jewish or Christian-monastic or Christian-arrogant it is. I see that a true Christian would feel differently, even a blurred Christian—such a one would not imagine it was an occasion for performance, or that one's performance would matter except as etiquette within a complex form of respect and a half-acknowledgment of one's own powers of being damned through disrespect and one's own silliness, a sense of one's twistedly complex and figural place in dozens of hierarchies, even of immortality seen as human effort stored in various ways—art and power —inside the giant tribe.

Or perhaps this is me as a prophet, as no one's son—i.e.,

a renegade from The World, an adherent of Faith, hiding it in a notion of *the Christian* and then saying I am not a Christian.

It is sad to know by how much a written account, removed from physical presence, fails. There is no equivalent in speech of the Seraphic appearance, no silence or stillness imposed by the dignity of what was seen and by one's wonder. The appearance of words on paper has only the unprovable presence of a sort of unhierarchical music and a black and white liberty of response; we speak to each other —honest listening is a form of speech—in a black and white republic of secrets and corners and silence in which what was present that afternoon is present in the language only if one is attentive and willing to be impressed or if some conviction concerning the subject and its meaning makes one patient or if some reputation of success and of duty and pleasure makes one attempt to attend the ceremonies of the music—otherwise, it seems the soul of the occasion is lost; and if it is not lost, it seems so mutual an act that in the light of the failure of language to be a presence, that the listener has spoken it in its truer form, the reader has written it with more faith and conscience—and workmanship— than the writer has written it although he tried but perhaps not full-heartedly enough; or perhaps the efforts of inscription dirtied things, and reading, or listening, is the purer and truer act, the better part of attention to the event.

I tried to keep my humor so that I would not faint. I did not want to not be present and fail the moment or have it be a dark moment and as far away as if I saw it through a veil of fever or other pain of the nerves as in lovemaking or writing or other forms of grace. I suspected that the initial courage of not fainting, of doubting and not doubting and being sane, would have to give way to a profound and unremitting awe sooner or later, which is to say, a madness of attention—I was more afraid of that than I want to admit—I was barely twenty—but I had my disrespect, my sentimental awe, rather than the real thing. At that age, to give way would be a limitlessly sexual surrender—and of a body young and of considerable common value and not yet greatly dirtied or misused. It was not profoundly surrenderable. I was proud still. Perhaps after torment or in certain kinds of ecstatic aggression, it would glide toward surrender—an outcry, a spilling; and I would *listen*. The silence would drain away and be full of sounds including that of my own freed voice—freed in this other—and not American—form. I had known some of the rapturous and tormented Berserkerhood of fighting and of earnest sports and of adventure, from which I more or less quickly returned to my usual forms of consciousness, rescued from adventure and mystic silence both, so to speak; but not yet having been broken by physical ordeals or psychological ones, by love or by ambition, and not having agreed to service in projects of acquisition or advancement or duties, I did not know the chains and secular horrors of prolonged intimacy with a manifest Truth as other people, more broken or less, in other patterns, knew about that stuff. Like any virgin, I wanted to set willful limits on whatever I did now—but only in the name of being strong enough for anything, a kind of boast that would not be proved out. My feelings of humor were a form of virgin independence, chastity, maybe obstinate—my lesserness was a great problem, you know? I said The Seraph spared us and did not speak—now, that is something I say, but when I try to imagine it not as a written fact but as a truth, I see it occurring second after second, in various forms of possibility and doubt, gambler's (and athlete's) odds, pretty much at the edge of an extreme surrender that the body yearned for and embraced and denied and scorned, and powerfully in each of those impulses or states; and the mind still more passionately within the frame of its own kind of passion, soared and fell, believed and waited—and had opinions, judgments even though I said earlier one didn't judge The Angel, one did; one gave assent and withheld it—well, it *became* clear that you had to do something, stand still and breathe, of course, then smile, salute, ignore The Angel, greet It, attempt to study It, love It, serve It in the face of Its gentle silence, its complete diffidence toward the real. Or one *should* rebel. It was clear (or rather it became clear) that Its Appearance was such that It did not need the assistance of language, or of patience. It was not a dubious object like The Serpent in Eden. It had nothing about it that was doubtful in the way ascribed to Angels sometimes in Holy Writ—It could command us in any way It chose, merely by a flexion of Its will, or if It had no will, then a flexion of Its thought, Its prayer, Its mode of song, whatever. The patience The Serpent had to show was necessary because its surface, its cold, legless glittery surface, its being a scale-y anomaly of a creature had to be overcome for the sake of persuasion; but the appearance of The Seraph as an example in the world, in Its own light inside the ordinary Boston sunlight, of nothing familiar in an altered and unfamiliar light was so self-proving, to say the least, or I was so persuaded, that It did not need to persuade us further—that was hardly the problem: I think assent without saying: I can't begin to describe the atmosphere of persuasion—but it was also a kind of big so what: We were persuaded—I want to say in the way light seems to be persuaded of itself, candlelight or sunlight—but we were given *no* instructions; and this was so extreme a feeling, so PROFOUND a feeling that I could not ever again doubt the extraordinary power of emptiness to be just about inevitably also a plenum of persuasion—of belief—and disrespect.

I understood, waveringly, how fame, the mania to build a palace, a pyramid, a book, how that male or human and female hunger to say *This Will Make History*, could rule one's life, to make manifest this mixture of will and belief and silence—and suitability and effect on others, as if forever: for as long as most things mattered to people. Mostly in real life I didn't feel that spur—for a lot of reasons—but I *saw* it now—a form of feeling it at a distance: Nothing could be more marvelous than to fill the earth with the reek of glory—but I was in need of the patience and charity and silence, the absence of ill treatment in The Seraph that afternoon at Harvard to feel that, to see it.

I have dreams of being like that. I can list elements of Its manner as I somewhat confusedly noticed them: a skin or integument or covering that was made of prisms or was sweaty and the sweat was prismatic. A hovering face-y-ness. Waterfalls, elephants (patience and strength), all manner of lightnings and glares, large and small flowers, rivers (of a lot of different kinds), children's faces in shadow in polite rooms, mirrors, explosions, plumages, grass, stairs, large (or monumental) doorways, and large and famous façades—It was of those orders of things visually but more *suitably, wisely*, more dear, more distant so that they probably ought not to have been named or listed as I have just done; it seems a childish list to me.

It was very fine throughout Its height and width and Its surfaces and in the implications of folds and pinions, gowns, wings, hands and the angle of its presumed neck and the unspeakable face which I do not have the courage yet to remember and probably never will, and which I may have largely invented because what I saw was not seeable, and I had these things, these forms, in me from other occasions and used them here.

The furthest extent of human perversity and independence of will was startled into good behavior, not completely, but to the point of attesting the miracle, the pause in natural law. No reporters or cameras got there, no one summoned further witnesses, it was a particular event, public but inward, and in the end private and without commotion or disturbance, except inside us, of course, those of us who were accidentally present, but, of course, I don't know what in the light of the nature of this occasion and of the Angelic Visitant the grounds of reason should be in speaking of an *accident* of presence.

The Seraph didn't try to register on us anything by way of words or gesture, re-written or explained commandments or biddings or forbiddings or predictions, none of those things. It didn't produce any *audible* effect except for a low hiss or whisper as of a fire. The tangles and fuzz of the human minds and sensibilities present, the ambitions—everyone, of course, was in mid-story, was in the middle of a dozen stories of enmity and friendship and of money and of circumstances and studies and love and family and politics

—we were in a sense let alone inside our stories. We remained unbidden, unspoken to, untrumpeted at.

At this stage, once past the initial internal uproar of seeing It and having to make room for belief that this was happening, it seemed incredibly loving and fond of It to say and do nothing, to let us alone.

Inside us, inside our skulls and bodies among the various *physical* devices of awe and caution (fear and attentiveness for observing) while being very shocked, some were like me, curious beyond the reaches or range of sense, good sense, while being somewhat unable to be disbelieving and amused (although in off seconds those feelings came anyway) and even drunk with relief in some instants because of having a conviction now of a final sense of importance about my life as a witness in this case, the actual case, the accident or fate or the luck or meaning of being present at this revelation—the revelation of the presence of an actual Seraph, no revelations so far in recent history having promised so much of the chance of a divine meaning separate from holocaust or apocalypse, although, of course, It might level us with fire or immediate oblivion now if it wished.

The idea that one might be incinerated or punished does bring in some people an illuminating burst of manners. Others, the women more, become hysterical at the implicit constraint. And one or two young men joined in with them in that. I was tempted by my own hysteria as well as theirs and verged on it but was reined, bitted, by upbringing and respect (the concomitant of disrespect in me) and curiosity.

And in a short time, the hysteria was quiet again.

It was stifled by awe, by the possibility of not having the

strength to endure all the kinds of weight of the occasion which is The End of The World but not entirely. The entire end, that would be A FinaMeanl ing. This had only a breath of a sense of Apocalypse, one not at our will; and it was Apocalyptic without any need of display in that the end of the world as it had been for oneselt one's death and the death of most of what one knew and the ways one knew it, the extinction of will in the old sense, of belief in the usefulness of will, occurred anyway, a kind of elicited asthma, self-annihilation, the birth of inhibition because of The Angelic Presence and Silence, A Silence that saw us, and if It did not choose to look, A Silence that was—since it was an undeniable presence—in an elaborate relation to us.

I imagine many of us to be such fighters that we try to hold onto certain advantages for dealing with what comes next even when what comes next is likely to be flame or more light than one can bear—perhaps it is impossible to give up one's nature at first or perhaps ever; one has one's strategies and appearance of virtue for the passage here, one's cunning, the Odyssean strengths at the vestibule to the Afterworld or within it, according to poetry, within the confines of Death.

Its presence, considering its speechlessness and power, was like *a death*.

But I imagined all that as laid aside with regret or even *hatred*, but since, if one lives, one will most likely be a witness from now on, what need is there for most of such aspects of will in one's self as one has needed up until now when one was not a witness? Almost certainly, one can expect to be inspired now and protected—oh, not physically: One can be martyred, used in various ways in whatever time or timelessness there is to be now: One has a very different sort of soul—the total of one's self now includes this occasion and one is different.

It was so impressive, The Seraph, that in the moments of seeing It, I had no wish to speak, to shout Alleluia or anything. Quite simply, there was nothing to say and there never would be now unless, of course, this was local, and one would want or be driven or inspired to speak of It to others who had not been here, who were absent from This Truth. At first, one or two of us did essay a casual *Hosanna* or *Alleluia* or *Hallelujah* or *Pax* or *Pace* or *Peace*, but it was like a mere further murmur and rustle of the leaves, of the air. After a while, no one shouted or cried out, every one of us, even a blind man nearby, we all forewent acclamation and the relief of outcry and of astonishment—we rested in an amused and *unresting* and exalted silence.

Then, that too passed in the lengthening pause or hiatus of the world, in this pause of our worldliness in which judgment, assent and dissent continued but not as before, those of us who remained sane and unhysterical inwardly and unrapturous in a total way, unbliss-ridden and as if in tears, and interested in dealing with others in this lengthening arch of time, of belief, glanced around at others on the walks to see if we were mad suddenly or if this moment was attached by the same approximate rules to the moments before as moments had always been attached to others. This was curiosity and disrespect, as I said, and unrestingness but not a restlessness of an exalted sort. Of course, moments couldn't be attached to each other by the *same* rules now, the rules that inhered in the moment before, of life taking place among us day by day, with breakfasts in it and bathroom acts and classes—but some of that did still obtain. One was not amnesiac. And the Heavens still had not opened to show The Ranks of the Seraphim and Cherubim and the Archangels, our Seraph had not spoken. What we had was enough even for someone greedy of spiritual glory but it was not the ultimate. In turning my head to look at what others were doing in the face of this unfinal magnificence, I did not deny that this was a rare moment, and in the light of final hope, the most rare moment in any recent age, matchless and singular, unspeakable and terrible, as I said at the start, this Marvelous Beauty and fearfulness and embarrassment—and it was not a night-dream, not a noon or late in the afternoon hallucination. But, unless it was those things after all, a dream or a hallucination, then, since I wasn't destroyed yet and the moment was real, I probably ought to attempt speech, now or soon, provided I hadn't been stricken dumb, speech as in prayer or greeting as I'd read men did in times of emergency or with Angels. I could question and plan, show piety (to some degree), praise, beseech, sing—it did seem that was what I ought to do next. I wanted to address The Apparition, The New Reality, and I murmured this and that phrase of salute and gratitude, *Hear, O Israel*, and *The Lord is my shepherd* and *Our Father* and, without intending blasphemy, *Hi, my name is Wiley*, but, of course, It would know. The language of ancient government, Latin, seemed more dignified, and I said, *Credo, credo*.

Part of me was freed from any urgency about manners or seriousness or awe ever again. One could testify by a kind of rough readiness since Salvation is inherently irresponsible once it occurs, if, that is, this was Salvation and not

Damnation, or something Entirely Neutral. But assuming from Its silence and the great beauty It had and from my continuing to live (although to be honest, I did not much care to live; I was grateful, though, and slightly sad or grated on by having my old consciousness) that what was occurring was kind, deeply so, well, one need not worry then, except, of course, as love or the spirit directs. The honest and for the moment and perhaps forever now monastic and martyrish soul, saved by visible presence, only that, is simple in spirit, like a child, one is a directly childish soul with a parent about whose judgment one is assured and about whose powers one has few doubts. In this state of trust, in this form, my will, as a fighter, if I may say that, led me to whisper, experimentally, out of an honest adherence to my own identity, my own soul, *My God* and *Hey* not exactly without and not quite with irony. I did contemplate, maybe with distaste, the impossibility of speaking of this later, this so obviously great happening: What could I say to anyone not present unless this event itself gave me a proper vocabulary for such an account?

But The Angel's silence supplied no clue to a language. How would one address the difficult auditory and intellectual apparatus for listening to me that people have? Here are the holes into which words drop and roll—and then unroll themselves into images—words and syllables; and here are the screens on which messages blink, jump, and are so radiantly tentative (while lyingly claiming supreme fixity and absolute reference); and here are fields and responses of electricity, electric bloomings and rustlings: One would have to organize a movement, have disciples and superiors and a kind of priesthood; the message has to be prepared for or it is entirely incomprehensible to the ears and eye and mind.

The Angel I saw did not speak because Its message was too corrective, too new: Its appearance had reference to Colossi and movies and other things. How could someone like me address such an apparatus as each modern man had for attending to speech or messages in reference to the truth of a vision like this one? People have their own knowledges insistently. Words, spoken or not, are by most educated people maybe brokenly re-created and read a second time, inwardly, and edited to replace what was said in accordance with what the listeners have already learned, and they have not learned this. Every man or woman listening to me is riffling through his or her past to find a former meaning or sets of old meanings to use rather than actually to listen to me. Or rather, they are listening to me in that fashion which means riffling through themselves to find old snapshots and records which they look at and listen to and say that that is what I mean. They have not learned what I now know—and I only partly know it.

And it was not certain that this was not The Last Trump, and that God Himself was appearing over Rome, say, more probably yet, Jerusalem, and we here in Harvard Yard were getting this outlying but impressive Local Show, a road show, A Local Angel, not The Central Figure but A Mighty Beauty anyway, and God would come to us later— that kind of old time and space notion seemed at once ludicrous and courteous—God acting like a man and being subject to a schedule and to time and space. How would one speak of this notion of Provincial Revelation and not be joking to the point of a painful inanity? Someone who had never had a Visitation or imagined such a thing or been given words and forms for thinking about it, what would he or she think, how could one convey the grandeur of a moment which omitted so many people, assuming they were omitted, that this wasn't the end of the world: *Don't look like that, Wiley, it's not the end of the world.* So many left unvisited, unvisioned, which somehow seemed unlikely, undemocratic—Elitist and selective—unjust—if this was an aspect of Deity, how would one deal with such injustice, accept it? We were privileged in The Yard—would that make one see one's life as a missionary effort, would one become finally evangelical, a matter of salesmanship and soul, perhaps of truth and bending the truth in order to serve The Truth? I had read of such things. It is hard to know and silly to speak of one's reactions honestly when they did not persist. Certainly I was conceited, and just as certainly I was modest. The moments did not continue being profound and my heart and soul were not steadily attentive to The Figure but often meandered or stumbled into delight or odd forecasts of the possible and a very great deal of hope about the future now as the silence of The Figure and my own continued life hinted that questions of meaning would remain.

For God is final meaning. And any intention of final meaning rests on thoughts of God. Any pure example, offered as purely true, hurls us skyward, halfway to the old Heaven. We in the West claim Divine Lineage for what we say and do and how we feel and act—not me: not me—and in The Figure and around it were such perspectives as cathedrals and theologies offer except there was no trace of Gothic or of columns and no symbol of theology that The

Figure carried. There was beauty and awe, a low hiss, great size, and a light that in spite of clarity and brilliance and beauty was mysterious—but this tone of order, Tacitean or Latin or whatever, was not present in the moment. Those of us who saw The Angel were not ennobled in any old sense of being invited—or forced—to be figures of a new government, of minds and of men and women—we were governors of nothing—but silence. Our testimony, I think I knew already, would be valueless except insofar as it was labored and worked on and logical, in some wholly logical sense, starting from an unideal premise, and having to admit that This Marvel, fine as it was, was not an Ideal Example of Divinity or of evil or of intrusion by Superiority—superior mind or whatever. One knew better than to claim the figure was Meaningless, that it had no Divinity or tie to Divinity—a claim of meaninglessness like that, or any such claim, like the claim to know or to have guessed at final meaning claims to know Deity and challenges the darkness. The Angel was silent. Why accuse The Figure then of meaninglessness? I did not turn my attention away from It for long. I did not stop desiring It. I did not begin to find it unsuitable. I did not turn my back to It and walk away. I remained there as long as It did. It was Glorious, It was the best I know about, but It was not Final.

And I used folly to rest myself from awe, from childish awe, perhaps it was childish, to rest myself from jealousy and jealous demand that It be more than It was or that It care for me more.

I thought even that perhaps some satellite system was in place and doing this; and Light and Electricity of no Divine Order would now flash from The Figure in front of me to underscore Its undoubted but obviously unclear meaning as a test or study of us: Or perhaps it was unclear only to me: But I did not look around to see how others were acting, I no longer had the courage to maintain a belief of my brotherhood with others—I said to myself that we all were fools and were being fooled and perhaps This was a mocking device of Extraterrestrials and The Military, but whatever way my nervous mind took at any forking or point of quandary, The Sight remained and so did my conviction of Its worth and meaning. The Seraph was so marvelous a structure that even if It were false, It didn't have to figure us out any more or do anything further or say anything: It had solved the problem of fooling me and taking over the center of my mind and heart just by being there in some incredible accident or plan which It seemed to have no intention of explaining.

Whereas I did have to do something. I had to speak to myself when My Awe or My Astonishment blinked. Self-preservation and pride reacted in their various automatisms when The Seraph refused to give a command, to display a sword or gun or trumpet, or to release salvoes of ancient or celestial fire, when It did not command me to be humble and to listen to Its silence, Its will, for which I was grateful since I would have tested Its Divinity or power in accordance with my systems for being a man here on this earth, in this life and might have been punished more than I was by knowing The Angel had shown itself without explanation or proof of divinity or purpose.

I know that I have to die like everyone else, and that displeases me, and I know every human born so far has died except for those now living, and that distresses me and makes most distinctions and doctrines look false or absurd or semi-absurd, but often I yearn to die, to have it be over, and then the doctrines look all right to me, and my own recklessness seems a verification of them, my folly proves them in part, by default: That happens up close to things and not at a distance; or rather, each state, of fear of death and of appetite for it is a peculiar mix of distances and closeness and of happiness and unhappiness.

To accompany The Seraph, to undergo the extinction of the earth in Its company, and my own extinction, to be forcibly seduced as by my father or my nurse or my mother when I was a small child, is a curious adventure to have as an adult. In just the way my father, S. L. Silenowicz, used to say, *We have to go inside now*, when we were out of doors together, The Seraph might take me out into the universe and dissolve my earthly self and make me into light or darkness at Its own will—it hardly mattered which: I could not sanely resist except in terms of silliness or inattention as a form of gallantry or as (along with obstinacy and the risk of bringing down punishment as a similar form of) flirtation with a potency so much beyond my own. The Seraph, by Its Presence, hoax or not since It was so impressive, announced the end of perhaps *all* my earthly pretensions; and It did this simply in the fact that It was There. It had arrived and become materially perceptible, and it remained materially perceptible, second after second, hoax or device of rule or whatever it was, and It did not care to cure the earth or me, time or light, although perhaps It touched with grace and final knowledge a number of minds but if so, the possessors of those minds have been secretive about it—nothing human so far possesses ultimate grace.

At most The Angel was an emissary of The Final but that was left to us, I think. I do not intend to re-enter the frame of mind I was in then. It existed in front of me, It had only to exist in my sight and as the major sweetness and crisply, almost burning center of the field of my attention, It had only to be There in Its Very Real Presence *in front of me*, for Its Literal Existence, Its True Presence to precipitate in me a changeable and varying conviction about many things and a Great Love for It, and This Conviction and This Love, this immense burden of meaning and awe loosened my self-control violently every few seconds, so that my inner state was one of varied heats of pieties, madnesses, catatonias, bits of peace, of grace, the varying convictions of Final or Real Meaning and of my struggles of will not to expect further moments and a return to silliness and doubt and emptiness—that is, my will still struggled to be a Will That Mattered and to be The Will that dominated my conscious existence—this even in The Presence of So Awesome a Will as that of The Seraph, or The Minds Behind The Seraph—and this came and went, these opposed heats and states of the soul, or states of mind, burningly and varyingly, like a flame, like one's heartbeat without seeming to have any nature of a paradox any more than one's usual heartbeat does—I mean one's own heartbeat, that variable and many parted, confers, with a reason, a rhythm, that a kind of invariable or unvarying meaning exists so long as my heart beats. One's own heart is a true heart, is true to one, one's own heartbeat is true, is my truth. Look here, now it is clamorous and now it slows; it is slowing but when one was excited, one's heartbeat, one's life, one's tidal nature were clearly present, the salt rush of blood truth, the taste of truth in one's mouth, the grownup taste of salt blood and heartbeat among fluctuations of heat and chemicals, the chemicals of sensation and of breath. I held my breath at times but I breathed, I had to go on breathing. I wasn't changed into a new order of man, although, to be fair, I expected to be. At times, I wasn't even changed into a new form of spiritual *amphibiousness* if I can say that, able to breathe and live in another medium besides the weekday one of ambition and cowardice and so on, the one I had chiefly known until now, but I had known another medium of awe and true docility although nothing that so breathed as this moment with the unbreathing Angel did of an actual eternity. In fact, my breathing—mine and that of one or two people near me on the college walk—seemed *pointedly* human, noticeably swoopish, gasping, and even asthmatic with nerves (or Awe) in comparison with The Seraph Who pointedly didn't breathe. And the oddity of the moment did seem to suggest we might be able to do without breath or might now be able to breathe in a new way, now that we were illumined or whatever, but it wasn't true, any more than I might be able to have the traits of my father or of an older brother merely by having a moment in which in my presence they prove their greatness of soul. I expected Its traits to be universal now, and I held my breath to see; and at one point, in simplicity of spirit, and at another time, with more complexity of mind, I half-rose on my toes and moved my arms to see if we (I and the others near me) could now rise in the air in final human pyramids, airborne, flocks of souls like grackles, humans in the absence of any story but this one now, going through the Aether to Heaven.

Or if that is too optimistic, to The Last Judgment.

Its Quality of Forbearance, of Distinguished Patience, had so much Meaning for me that I had no real doubt that It was A Manifestation and not a hallucination, that it was a phenomenon of lived existence, a phenomenon of lived theology and goodness, not a trick that could make It be of No Meaning except a human meaning of ruse or whatnot.

Indeed, I thought that was Its purpose, so much so that I did not fear my humiliation at Its will, I did not think it a policeman of any kind, or a messenger exactly, so much as a marker. I accepted it, my humiliation in relation to It, which you could say was at Its will, at Its permission, in an (if I can boast) burst of being civilized: I wasn't what it was; and it seemed ugly, even blasphemous, both as human stuff and toward the divine to assert myself: it is enough, I have had a chance to see It.

But that sounds as if I were living out a pattern of being a younger child or some kind of scholar with a balanced wit or wit of balance and I'm not like that, and the moment was not like that. I was not at the center of Its Attention but no drama and no testing inhered in that—the quality of Divine Speech, of mattering as an equal to the Divine Loneliness, if such a thing in some form exists, is a long way off and involves many more kinds and depths and heights of metamorphosis than puberty and death. Purpose is really an odd thing, a very odd thing. The Angel made no request for affection or service, It did not exemplify or ratify any human dream in the sense of what one dreams for oneself except in being not like us and closer to The Great Power or The Great Illumination.

I could not know if I was shrewd enough or intelligent in piety or the most severely black-souled and sinful or what

—if It had a message, it was that silence, that one of not choosing anyone. Since It didn't speak, it was easy to feel It hadn't chosen us—we were a random sample. Beauty and goodness may very well, from a higher point of view, be matters of accident, defending and preserved, or sung about; and they may very well test you first of all by being uncertain in themselves as to their nature and, secondly, by giving you no answers. You mimic and sing the best you can and try to become someone whose life makes a music of a sort you can admire; or you had best stand still and mimic the silence of The Angel since you cannot reproduce a quantum of Its beauty or Its silence.

I was given nothing and I was given everything, I was not tested, I was too much tested, the test would continue the rest of my life now that I had seen This Thing, provided life continued. I was not the most just or good or the most obstinate or the most sly (or sly at all in Its eyes, Its view) among those who were present or was but *it was not known*. I was not the median or the worst. None of that was at issue. Its light made me blink in such a way that it was as if I stared even while my eyelids were lowered—I don't mean the light was oppressive or insistent; or that it interrupted the darkness with its bright oddity: It interrupted everything by Its presence but only in the way you don't escape from someone you're infatuated with—their mind and presence—and this was inwardly so now for me, that I had been given The Sight of the Thing. I saw steadily inside my own identity now even when I blinked inside, even while I tried to rest from, escape from, attentiveness and Awe. As in any romantic situation, my flirtatious or gallant and damnable silliness, my more and more straining nerves, my sense of meaning and of my being chosen, my rising to a new condition of mind, my being named and at the same time forsaken, my New Love kept me in an excited state and on the edge of folly—but I didn't do as some men there and some women did, I didn't start talking and claiming to be the mouthpiece of The Spirit.

No one listened—you had The Thing Itself right there. You didn't listen to more than a word or two, you could tell from the faces those people were no help—what's the point of hiding inside Error? I would rather be openly wicked—inattentive—jolly.

I mean, the talkers were duplicitous, were hypocrites: They were playing with damnation after it was fairly likely The Angel had not brought death or salvation. Perhaps by implication, by presenting us with a speechless premise, which, if no one appeared with a television camera, if this occasion could not be proved to have occurred, would have to be argued over and socially dealt with, absorbed, socially digested, turned into an issue, another one, all our lives, and after we were dead, depending whether another manifestation occurred or not. But meanwhile these feverish souls, unable to regard The Marvelous Thing, were talking, were arguing about Its nature, were claiming to know Its nature, were making offers in Its Name—it was sad, that part of it.

One or two other people spoke intelligently—they testified to Its silence and to Its beauty, to the fragile commonness of the event—they wanted to know if others saw something of the sort they saw, and I thought each thing they said was of immense beauty, but then some of the chatter about Heaven and Hell The Seraph had supposedly

whispered to those other minds was beautiful to me too—
but these two people, a man, a woman, each of whom said
only things such as, "It is silent," and "I don't know what
to think," and "Isn't it beautiful? You could never build a
church that would testify to such beauty—do you think It
wants us to try?" seemed to me more remarkable than the
things about Heaven and Hell, which, also, as a matter of
truth, I believed while I listened.

While I listened, I felt, I guess, it was in sympathy to
the speaker, some part of my own consciousness of belief.

The effect of Its Height, of Its Colors and Their Extraordinary Nature and Their Changeableness and The Exceed-
ingly Plangent Pleasure It gave by The Sight of It, did so
ornament the burden—and extend it—the half-dear and
agonized onus of recognizing that the event had meaning
and that The Meaning of This was not given to us in any
simple way, Its beauty eased our condition at living now
with no Final Meaning of This Manifestation, and in no
absolute condition of Testimony that it was almost all, all
right, but not really.

It didn't judge, It didn't raise a sword or other weapon
or even Its Hand, It spared us Its speech, and if It spoke to
us, did so by inducing thoughts inside us, and yet, if my
case is that of others, those thoughts, too, were uncon-
trolled. Years of shame at my inept powers of attention, at
the vagaries and caprices of mind when it, the mind and its
cohorts, the other horses (or motors) of consciousness,
sensing and instinct so-called and what's called heart and
what I call physical will, those forms of consciousness, in
ordinary states or raised up by discipline and grace, had

always meandered and reared and run away and never were *chemically* or animally exact or mechanical.

Nor were they now raised—or inspired at all—a little, because of happiness and awe—an allowed coltishness and what seemed instinctual caprice, chemical caprice, mild or greater devilishness interfered. In fact, all the attributes of mind were present now, inside me, but were soothed by the absence of fire and anathema or any sign of wrath or lightning. It was not a matter so much of *The Mildness* of The Figure as it was of Its *Tender Otherness*—no war, or antagonism of a great sort, even in the love, existed, since I could not speak for It or embrace It—such a moment was so far off.

I had known moments of love and goodness and beauty and this moment was much, much less up and down than those but not very certain. The Sheer Otherness toppled me —balked me. It was not flesh or stone or any regulated kind of light or any known anatomy or architecture of *the human* that I now loved and regarded, nothing that humans had known, no sunset light or movie light. It was not any recognizable thing. Except, of course, It started—no, no— I mean It offered starting points of recognition: bits of recognizable light, a suggestion of hand and arm and chest; and you went from there to recognition, or I did. But I could not see myself in It or imagine It as related to me in any way but that of superior power or perhaps of Its Hiddenness as A Personal Reality on the other side of a metamorphosis that was not occurring at this instant, that was not bringing me any closer to the possible thing of It and me embracing each other at least partly by *my* own will.

Just as being a man had been hidden from me on the other side of the sharp ridge of puberty when I was still ten years old, so The Angel existed on the far side of a metamorphosis involving Beauty and Goodness, strength and knowledge, that would never happen, but that I would dream about, or edge close to in moments of grace now, although I was quite sure I would not be able to remember The Angel because my memory, my mind hasn't the ability of my senses to regard something for which I have no formal means of interpretations and retention. To be granted grace —or to have been someone who has stolen grace—is no final state: Part of its definition is that one has no formal means of identifying or summoning it, only of guessing at its presence and speaking later of its occasion. I don't know. The effect of imagining or sensing now that I was *not* going to undergo a metamorphosis in that sense, that I was not going to become like It and in any way equal to It and able to control Its attention or admiration, made my mind wander and made me love It as I might have loved an older brother had he been of any worth but, of course, much more than that but considering my wickedness and pride and my common sense, since I was so excluded, the love was hopeless, even in the terms of my own dreams, it was not a final love.

Along with the other things I felt, which I felt inconstantly, as I am trying to describe now, this was, oh, a factor in suggesting the possibly *universal reality of rebellion* —disrespect as making itself into truth—even into revelation. Revelation has in it two themes, one of deprivation and one of acquisition: inferiority to the ideal and even to the best of one's own possibilities of attention, and on the other hand, revelation granted you an imperial grace or role, the means toward the acquisition of Grace and Meaning, or at least, knowledge of it, a sense of its place in one's kingdoms or nearby.

But there could be no peace because of It, no cessation of motions of the mind or of the hurt and self-consciousness and arduous labors of will and of Love.

And since The Seraph did not organize us—an army or, more beautifully, a choir—or change us frighteningly as suppliants with torn faces and fire and ashes and risen bodies and the dead around us and rending noises, the soul at Judgment—one could see how revelation brought no unison and only the most complex imaginable forms of union and this probably would not have changed even if The Seraph had asked us to line up and sing—unless It had transformed us first. The brotherhood I felt toward the other bystanders was mitigated by embarrassment which, lo and behold (if I might say that), had to do with competition and shame, with rank in terms of behaving well, or seeming to, those who seemed to know what to do and feel, those who had risen to the occasion and those who hadn't, grace in my Gentile sense of things, and also a competition about the fiercely scoffing egalitarianism and consequent contempt for us all in our pride and identities (since we are interchangeable) that was at that time my most essentially Jewish trait—this led to a sense in me of struggle, which I denied in the moments of peace, but whether denied to be such or not, the moment of revelation was individual with only limited aspects of being shared.

But those were very beautiful—the sharing part.

But even The Pleasure It gave by The Sight of It or the

fear It aroused or themes and thoughts of Holiness and Awe, these were not universal even among us, at least not noticeably so at any one time. What was *universal* among the fifty-eight watchers in The Yard and on Massachusetts Avenue according to later studies were things that could be called Awe but two people denied having had any sense of holiness at all. Massachusetts Avenue was at once renamed The Street of Universal Light and the street was rebuilt to form The Square of the Seraph but when the struggle between, on one side, the Irish and black officials of Cambridge and Boston and Massachusetts and those of Harvard, was won by Harvard, the whole thing was considered not a folk phenomenon, but something for the educated classes —this is my own lifetime that I am talking about.

Certainly, for a while, religion ruled at Harvard after this; one might call it a fashion, religion being more important than the state—the state being slowly moved toward being theocratic—but that was something brought by people who had not been present.

What I saw was a special event that did define the state as secular. The Final Meaning that many of us hungered for had little to do with the politics of daily stuff. I myself would much rather be Holy than Secular—I mean in the world—but in some form other than an insect-like union or a vast and regimented family of sons, say, or of wives, or all of us as wives, male and female alike, or all of us husbands married to a truth that is so unclear in purpose as the one of The Apparition that day.

Some of us expect a union of souls and Meaning which will be both clear and simple, and more than either of those, Final and unarguable—each man, each woman, a key, an

explanation, a Thrust of Holy Will—and some of us *feel*
that way now but not sensibly, not based on *evidence*, more
as a matter of practical will, staying alive, loving one
another to the degree that that can be managed without
hypocrisy.

This wish in me bled that day with consistent wounding.
Each stab, each cut came from more evidence at the complexity of *Truth* in seeing The Seraph stand and maintain
Its silence. The spirit sank and was wounded and pale at
the trigonometry-like extent of any answer or response,
moment after moment, second after second.

And like the shadow which I still cast on the walk and
which lay in the air between me and the ground, a granu-
lated semi-lightlessness that had the shape of an irregular
pyramid so that when I think of my eyes and consciousness
near the top of the pyramid, I think of the figure on the
dollar bill of the pyramid and eyes. The desire for simplicity and a portable and easily mentioned answer cast this
shadow of my will—this attempting this account—this attempt at meaning, at mattering.

I cannot bear The Seraph's Message, I cannot exemplify
It or Them, Its messages. If It had spoken, I could not now
reproduce Its Words, Its Diction, Its Authority. I suppose
part of me had always known that a sense of Failure must
accompany any attempt at Truth, that satisfaction can never
reside in an answer but only in the politics—or warfare—of
answers as the Greeks knew, as appears in those famous
plays—but still I felt a curiously profound shame, an increasing embarrassment, it seemed to me that there was
more shame and shamelessness now that The Seraph had
appeared, more than I had imagined could exist, and an

increasing embarrassment among some of those under-graduates present who were struck dumb and some who were struck senseless and some who were struck giddy from the strain of a continuance of honest knowledge of how limited and silent knowledge is—ever and always.

It is easier to take a small formulation and lyingly—and honestly, too—use it as an amulet or whatever to stand for a bigger amount of truth and to say that that is THE WHOLE TRUTH than to use a large amount of truth with all that labor and still have to admit that it's only partial and needs correction.

That day, those who became giddy and giggly and who took the soldierly persistence, the Immediate Depth of Belief, of the more serious starers and watchers and tautly awed head-averters as authority for the reality and value of what was occurring saw that the more serious in some cases passed out or rose from the kneeling position when their knees began to hurt. Others scratched themselves or looked suddenly tired or doubtful. Some, not shockingly under the circumstances, actively pursued sexual shame, sexual release, like temple harlots, men and women, because their minds and hearts had been set that way, probably by chastities they practiced; they offered this to The Seraph, or they did it out of greed to taste the excitement of it or in case it was the last one or as offerings of themselves or as disrespect or as a way of claiming attention as some children do with trickily obscene or dry parents or by association of ideas as a form of honesty and of abnegation of the world and its rules concerning shame and self-protection. Well, I have said all this in a confused way. But again it was clear that no actually universal or regimented reaction occurred among us, even the small group of those fortunately present here today, this afternoon. We had a great variety of responses in ourselves and in others around us. At some point, two people began to dance, far apart from each other. One man disrobed and stood with his hands over his breast and his elbows out and he looked very dour and sure of the holiness of this; and a woman with a powerful voice began to sing but she soon stopped. But then two other people began to sing, but different hymns, and then one changed and sang the other's hymn, and the strong-voiced woman joined in, the three sang for a while, less than a minute, I think—it just wasn't one of those times for showing off in that way even though that wasn't showing off, really.

I tried to sing but I was off-pitch as usual. I was shocked and a little irritated that I was not inspired in a vocal way—it bothered me that I was not raised into the air. It bothered me that we were not joined in a choir, that we were not enjoined to be a group, I began to cry and I got a headache. And the headache and the tears altered in nature and were purgative or oppressive by turns, complaining and merely nervous, joyful and meaningful and then not—this was as time passed.

The witnessing was eccentric, and hardly admirable, what we noticed and how we showed off, and the way we stared and did not stare. There was belief and various ways of enduring and attempting to recognize what was in some regards stupid—It was too magnificent—It had been suitable at first, in getting attention and governing our regard, but we had adjusted in various ways, or failed to adjust, which was partly unbearable, and no further uplift of will or of display or of realized fantasy occurred, and a lot of us wondered how we were to live.

I was in favor of our being raised into the air and of our becoming an amazing choir, and failing that, our marching to downtown Boston in mid-air, or failing that on the ground, in the name of the Truth and with the perhaps grandly ambulating and accompanying Figure Which might, though, have refused to move, Which remained in Cambridge right there, at Harvard Hall.

We might have circled it like the Jews the walls of Jericho or David the Ark.

But no, we stood there—now some people sat—It continued to give no message, It continued to exist in front of us, and that made the structures of will necessarily docile and responsible, which was grating but which was, in other regards, an ecstasy like other occasions I had known although not so gloriously as this. A serious kind of ecstasy, grave and unexpected, at least by me. The effect of thrumming modesty and immodesty that The Seraph evoked in me (I can say that as if that effect had been constant if I pretend I exhibited no variations of reaction) was a matter of a very precarious sense of brotherhood or equality with It, or of descent, as in blood descent or lineage, in that I seemed to myself to mirror It or know about It to any degree—that knowing made it seem to me I comprehended It—one loses track of how ignorant one was when some terrific knowledge or other is glowing there in the forefront of your consciousness; and this sense of union with a great force, a greater force than any I had imagined as showing Itself on earth, carried me toward a swift, terrible pride and delight in the human availability of such a grand inhumanity of spectacle, the specialness, the half-inhumanity of It now that It was somewhat familiar, the way Its Colors and Shapes overlapped suddenly what one knew from one's own experiences in life and of representations of the ineffable, maybe, so that one as if *recognized* in It light itself and the size of night, as well, and starry numbers and grandeurs of air and vistas, and then the way It, Its Colors and Shapes departed while It stood there, departed from my powers to see, perhaps, the way It became phenomenally ghostly, like speech, conceivably present, but not present, imaginable and said but mostly absent, a whisper, an echo, a hint, this had a gravely incremental effect of ecstasy, which in my case became a kind of illiterate eloquence inside me, a babbling, a glossolalia of childish and dream rhetorics—I had been freed from certain human restraints, I was free to be insane—human restraints were mostly absent in the presence of The Angel, It overrode them, satirized and splintered them—and I was not insane in relation to It, the light; by my own or private standards I was allowed to have been adopted by the moment, if you follow me, and to testify in my own blur of languages, in my own meanings, which part of me quite clearly understood and welcomed as being poetry and music but I know now no one around me could have recognized much of what I said except insofar as it was ecstatic and self-concerned but directed to The Angel as release and as offering.

It was there but in such a way that seeing It was as if Its passage or the passage of Its attributes among us was on some orbit of Mere Being, and our specialized and ignorant responses seeing It, or not seeing It, our accepting It, our testing It, was A Truth and Necessary but peripheral to the other watchers and could not possibly matter to The Angel Itself.

It was painful but harder on the believing Christians who are convinced God deals in the details of our existence in memory of His Son. For me, a Jew, I writhed with powerlessness, I ached at the complete humility Its presence forced on us in relation to meaning itself. We could not possess It or treasure It or distract It or own It or guess Its will: We were given no power at all—but none was taken from us either, except the power of a certain kind of conceit, of not knowing The Angel existed. We were given or granted irresponsibility, silliness, enormous possibilities of dutiful sonhood and subservience in a sense, but we were given none of the ancient or antique power to *command* God through His Son or His Covenants.

We were not like It, we were not cousin to It in the realm of matter and mind and the possible dignities of soul and vision, we were secular and strange and minor, we could mirror It as children do adults at times, and that was to show madness, lunatic attempts at private meaning, silliness, to a grownup immersed in a silent passion and meaning, I guess.

It Itself was irrelevant and gray and transparent for entire moments as one's state changed, as thoughts involved one in slow chains of inner recognition and outer curtaining to the world. If I wish to remember Its Light, which was more a shadow, really, a displacement of the only light that had been familiar to me until now, Its peacock and flaming sun and star and moon and flower and garden and winter colors-of-a-sort, I remember a partial reality of Its Presence intruding on my thoughts, on my confused rhetorics and outswell of honest syllables, how I was corrected when Its Colors returned or when I re-fashioned and re-sharpened my vision since The Angel's colors were, of course, ungraspable by the mind or memory, the many-fingered, hundred-handed mind. The unfingered but shoving memory had no chance. Memory shoves things forward, but only the mind can hold or handle images, can study them. Memory can show things to me as I understood them once, not usually in their presence, but in an early memory or daydream or dream at night, that's all it can do.

Brotherhood has odd passages of deadness toward one's brothers in it. One's brothers, a stricken audience—but not entirely, if at all.

They matter, one's brothers do; they prove me sane, that this is actual—the communal mind judged this to be perceptible.

Under the circumstances of Its silence, should we worship It? Well, not compete or intrude or ask things of It—except gingerly.

One graduate student in English threw a rock at It; and an Oriental physicist attempted to sketch It, to stand both in Its Light and safely behind a tree and look at it from there as if to triangulate Its Height or Quality, which was impossible since It has no shadow, no ordinary relation to Light or, consequently, to dimension or time.

Free Will continued to exist in the very face of the Divine, the Divine on this order at least, but it was Free Will partly shameable by our being Middle Class, our training in *Respectability*, in self-willed conformity, self-willed facelessness, law, democracy or smudged holiness or piety.

Historically, God and the middle class are at odds, or I would guess the middle class hasn't produced theology. Comfort and decency aren't much like grace and the non-elect, aristocrats and the poor. Our God would supply universal shelter and would go easy on the punishments since we were trying and would be less severe a figure and hardly doctrinaire—I really can't imagine a feudal theology in a suburb. Or at Harvard. Or in a poem except as a ludicrous—but beautiful—term about one's own success in the now more and more middle class world—the world is the human universe, really.

Many of us asked things about It of It silently, but we obeyed the call to politeness issued by the phenomenon and our own allegiance to *decency* in some cases and our allegiance to celebrity and specialness in other cases—The New Higher Respectability and Fashion of the Soul—since great power suggests coercion and, partly, makes disrespect noble by making it expensive, as expensive as Respectability, at which point it has in it clear responsibility toward meaning.

To some extent, we surrendered a great deal to The Seraph, we were mostly not disrespectful—like dogs. So, we did not hate each other's ill-timed disrespects very much so far as I can judge now. The sketcher stopped sketching very soon. The rock-thrower stood very still in the pale, strong, low-lying altered light around The Seraph.

That fierce and terrible and altered light, what weird geometries of hints of pinions and limbs the Seraph displayed in slow pale and then brilliantly colored semi-fluttering. It was like nothing else—of course. Thank God.

I was humble. There He-It is. I had felt as a matter of

personal doctrine that God would not bother with a manifestation, nor would The Devil—or any demon either—why should Power bother with mediation or an image when It can do and be The Thing? It can impose unspeakable bliss, unspeakable belief in us, horror in the mind as well as in the air, horror or charity in the act. A Power would be not merely greater than life and death—we have that power with tools in one case and will and belief in the other—but A Power would be more insistent than life or death which no man or woman yet can be.

Unless A Power exists but is not omnipotent and must consider the economics of Its Acts, the politics of sheerly animal truth in making Itself apparent to us and in us finding It out as apparent. I could not see why It should be so patient. Men mostly did demand they be recognized as having access to the Divine and that they spoke in Its name and with many or all of Its privileges—the idea of The Divine was an Idea of Impatience. I 'knew' The Seraph was bullshit—as was, therefore, my pain concerning It, my awe and longing about It, my silliness, my bliss—it was like a dream of happiness slowly making itself known as a dream. Some human had to have dreamed it up. The real and its politics were about to return. It was just flattery to believe The Superhuman would bother with us. I envied the wit, the malignance and magnificence in the knowledge of Goodness, and the obliquity of the jokester, perhaps the groups of jokesters, who had imagined and vivified the image, The Imagined Messenger-thing and set it here, who had caused it to appear to me *and others*. Deity can't be transcendence of Itself toward the human—can't need us or care unless it too is finite—not final. The Angel did not transcend Itself for us. The Seraph in a lower sense transcended itself by suggesting Heaven and a message—the stillness of utter safety, of no further hunger of any sort. Only a trick would move me toward God in a human—or comprehensible—way. I am moved by Deity that cannot speak to me, that strangeness, that foreignness as yet so unlike us, something beyond what I can or can't know, nothing of It lies within the procedures, the progression of the moments, now, and the ones before, and the ones to come, and the jolted and erratic groups of images of them in memories—God and This Angel are the final points of acknowledgment for me, me, Wiley, who can say, in a case like this, only yes or no, Yes I see, No I will not grieve. A binary form, A Binary Fact—perhaps a chain of sets of binary fact, my religious belief: It is True or It is Not True—but I will believe much that I don't otherwise believe if it is understood I believe it for the sake of brotherhood. But Deity for me is a fact without presence to which I say Yes or No. It is present or not present, It is felt or not felt, known or not known—it is always felt and is not known inside the human range, only in human terms. This form of agnosticism, if it must have name, means I can't conceive of a Transcendent Truth but only of truth and falsity and sloppiness in a mix—I can't imagine what a final truth would be in actuality. Those who speak of such a thing say it is not apparent, it is colorless like glass, it is a radiance that lies beyond things, it is summonable by magic, by incantation, by acts named as virtue, it is known by faith. Some say it is apparent. It is referred to in words and known in the heart and passions, apparently, but it is not present beyond those words to me, and it does not enter my heart and my passions. I saw merely a local Seraph that enjoined a respect toward the real as a kind of exile and honor and as disrespect and fear toward the silences that exist in meanings. It bade me love incomplete meanings and with my whole heart but only for a while. It told me to be fickle. It said—It did not speak but I say *It said*: You see how I lie, how I twist things—It said that only new positions are honest or possible but they ebb into old ones, into ghostliness and confusion (a tradition is what one remembers from one's childhood, one's grandparents, say—a living tradition is never more than twenty or thirty years old). It said that differences could not be escaped from, politics were inevitable, that political meaning is out of place in relation to real power, genuine beauty, true silence or speech, but they will occur then anyway. It said to abjure tyranny as much as possible and if that meant having many gods, do so, but to recognize that anarchy was weak. It said to love incomplete and complex meanings and One Speechless and apparently not Omnipotent God and to struggle toward a new idea of idea, therefore.

The Seraph I quote, who never spoke, is not present beyond these words. It was never present for a second except as revelation to the eyes and senses in great and even dreamlike power and richness—that abundance in solitude, inside one's head. I speak of It now as a vicar of Its absence. I serve in the vicarage of absence. What I am is a man of service in a reality that has degrees of truth and of presence.

Deity is Itself. *Transcendence* would be, logically, a term for us cheating on A Final Awe—it would be a trespass. A final awe, even uncapitalized, is hard to practice. Nothing was transcendent in The Angel's appearance, actually—Its presence was merely, or not so merely, the presence of meaning—meanings complex and not as yet known, and the knowing of which is without set value, and cannot be enjoined as a duty. I was humbled as I have often been—I gaped, I did not claim then or ask to be a leader or Messiah but then only a few short men did in The Angel's presence. No one was able to misrepresent or to speak for The Manifest Meaning when it was present. One lies later for the sake of being audible and triumphant. To speak to fools as a good hostess does, does Deity authorize a foolish manifestation?

That was beyond me. I thought of what the image cost. I thought of what such a grand image cost in the universe. I was always broke and I didn't have the money to do anything even moderately splendid except in my sleep. I couldn't help thinking of money. I had never dreamed of so splendid a spectacle as this. I could see that some churches and temples ought to be made of gold, dangerously I mean, if they want to suggest belief or faith really: The final commitment of all that is material to the appearance of divinity shows that the community is serious in what it says about God, is what I am saying, I suppose.

It towered up, a structure of light but palpable like and unlike the church of light the Nazis made at Nuremberg, and maybe more like the statues of Athena and Zeus that Phidias did of ivory and gold at Olympia and Athens, which were painted as unearthly flesh which was apparently weird with divinity as in the curious light and colors and scale of dreams—but this was wakeful, this was very wakeful. Or at any rate, so people said who saw those manifestations. The Zeus was one of The Seven Wonders of the Ancient World.

This Seraph in front of me was not the work of a dead artist in another state of soul, other from mine. This one I envied. Do you love or respect anyone who's alive? To the point of self-obliteration and awe? I suppose in prison or in hospitals, in certain states of anguish of soul, some people do. At any rate, I envied the creator of This Angel and was in awe still, was still plucked at by love and a wish to be Good—this was toward the end of the manifestation and I had a headache and considerable nausea and an erection.

I could not imagine who could live and create such an illusion, the reality in front of me. Surely, the creation and the ambition involved would manipulate the Creator. Much of what I have witnessed in my life, all that I have witnessed, I have resented at times, at one time or another. My having to see it was hard to bear, my having to return to the thought of it later was still hard, too—maybe worse. Witnessing is a terrible duty, a kind of horror—especially the witnessing of otherness and of incompleteness, which is what witnessing is as we know in life. Self-love alternates with confessions of ignorance, and selflessness, in a difficult way. I was distended by The Sight of The Angel. When I do not violate my knowledge of It by claiming to have found a final truth about It, I become so charged and swollen with vision that I go pretty far toward being lunatic. And the pain of that and of the extended effort to speak is silencing, is very great. But I can't say I would have preferred seeing nothing. Or even that I would have preferred seeing indirectly, on the face of someone, not me, what happened, rather than undergo the act of witnessing the stuff myself and being a conduit for such things as the joke or farce of the at-times-ghostly, at-times-glass-mosaics-in-sunlight angel and then its ghostly avatar in gray, in a single color in myriad shades again. I can't say seriously what I would prefer, less beauty, more beauty—this is what happened. Clearly the truth of it lies in the moments, not in my opinions. My opinions, though, hint at what occurred, they hold evidence together in abbreviated form, but it is incomplete evidence. It is troubling, however, and it takes too much time to open each case, each trial again. I am so broken and burnt with the effort of resurrecting and of continuing and containing the unuttered messages of this event, which admittedly was not ordinary, but it was, in its nature of abstraction infinitely easier than an event involving people on both sides, both with power and arrival and messages and departure. The human messages seem to me to be much harder. But The Seraph's arrival and the messages of that and their lasting or twisting into messages implicit or otherwise of duration and their going on afterward in me, the memory even during the time of the visible manifestation, during the moments of the reality of Its presence, I can almost say I am not to be trusted any more than if I were testifying about what I saw in a brawl or an act of murder. I admit that often while It was present, before It vanished, I was sarcastic and angry, cheap and self-destructive and stupidly thrilled, knotted with obstinacy and reluctance because what was going to happen was so commanding a fate that I preferred to be evil or foolish or wasteful in order to be slightly free. Will is so strange a substance, so willful, so self-blinding that I felt bullied and shoved either way, whichever way I went. But, of course, Awe returned and gratitude, the real kind, the kind that at moments is not embarrassed, after a while, of my having been mean-spirited off and on or always during the course of the manifestation in relation to an ideal of some sort, and of the certainty of my being it again.

I could not have left Its presence. I don't think many people could have left Its presence without first having the capacity to be vastly bored: That would free them to their willfulness. Or the conviction that it was overall a lie and oppressive, and most likely, an act of Mammon, something done for money in the service of a god who was a servant of Unrighteousness, some such thing—I was immersed in Its moments, the thickets and plain fields of meaning—of meanings. As I said, I regretted my presence—I regret my testimony now—I keep thinking to myself, Wiley, don't get lost, don't get too humble, you have the moments. To guide me, I mean. I can almost say I regretted it but maybe in the end I'd rather not say it because it isn't perhaps true enough. What can I regret or prefer in the face of The Real? In a way, it is wrong, or impossible, to speak of The Seraph's vanishing. The nature of its presence changed, became more human, more subject to absence as if much of one's humanity was based on absences, too, on memory and its showiness in its display of things.

The particular drama of the departure of The Real Angel, of Those Colors It has, and Its Odors of flame and darkness—and of light—and Its Faint Whisperings and low whistlings and humming sounds, was mixed with the unexpected and untimely appearance of the Moon, a sudden silver rose that showed itself in the dusky air, large and unlikely and at treetop level—a sudden dizziness of the zodiac, of time. Perhaps an illusion based on misperception of what the passage of The Angel away from me, from us, was like, and how that energy played in the universe and in the immediate and local air, as well, and how it illuminated the darkness with extensions of the angelic colors. And these were spread everywhere among the trees and over the buildings whether they faced us or not—one knew because the light showed at the corners, too, and on grass behind them, light, shadows, outlines and surfaces washed in—so to speak—the shallows of this light, at this shore of an ocean of the universe's capacity for further light; but it was as if the Seraph had never been there but was now present in this mixture of sun and moonlight, auroras, and unseeable lyricisms of illumination, as if memory and opinion might invent new colors that would color the world outside and the poor eye among its lashes and with its retina would try to deal with this and would be as happy as a child feeling foolish at the seashore seeing something marvelous washing in the waves, in the shallows but understanding nothing of it, not the light, not the salt smell, not its own happiness. Memory and opinion and the new colors then existed briefly according to new laws, different laws; and this illumination was partly a mirage of a sort common at dusk, but that was a hallucination: One doesn't see dawn at dusk or associate sunset hopefully with ideas and sensations of dawn—one suggests thought and rest and one suggests actions and waking from the megalomaniacal selfishness of dreams—dreams and error, self-love and fear. In this magical dusk one might think of gathering with others at dinner as if at home, but also as if at dawn right after waking or after a vigil. To wake taut from sleep and dreams, from dreamed crowds and the actual solitudes of sleep, and to return to a moment centered on family or on colleagues, these domestic and *selfish* moments, are ones in which one regards oneself as favored by Deity or in disfavor, in combinations of luck and will and errors or not-errors and accident and not Deity or whatever—responsibilities, laws, the day, the night—somehow us partly in the grace of the illuminated All-Powerful. Perhaps I was wedded to myself for a fraction of second, and in that blink, in that slow-witted, human, disobedient act of *my* self-regard—in the way a child blames itself for having brought on the eclipse by turning on a light switch that he was not supposed to touch—The Angel already visually forgotten by me stopped being there.

It hardly made a difference at first. Everyone (I think all the watchers) waited, not knowing what to expect or to hope for next. What came next was simply a somewhat sluggish return to a usual afternoon light, a Yankee sobriety of Massachusetts glare at 4:06—approximately—it was not clear at what moment It was gone, and some people were crying and others were carrying on somewhat, and that was distracting. I was bathed in the afternoon's ordinary river of white light, yellow light, its faint heat and the damp coolness near the ground and struggling to grow, an invisible harsh corn, into the ice fields of winter.

A dead edge of cold's in this air, an autumnal vinegar—in my salad days: a joke. The cold is smooth, this mixture of heat and cold is like the rough feel of a cat's tongue. I feel the Cambridge damp as pale, always pale, a thin, decaying heat, a near lightlessness. Darkness comes on. I am in a thinning, fraying light. Vague mist, like lint, lies among some distant buildings in the perspectives here and among or near some of the trees. The restlessness of ordinary time lies between me and the adventure and the vanished light. The Seraph. There is only a make-believe point of stillness, an illness perhaps, a frozen affection, a passion of study and of concentration, to suggest any timelessness to crawl into or to climb on in the attempt to know what happened. Hustled by real time, I am filled with a kind of hushed rage of thought, spilled and quiescent, spilling and restless: *What does it mean?* When I was young, I lived in a pulsing urgency of thought, thought as flame or bone and blood unless I was in the sun or busy at a sport. It was a kind of rage of thought. It's hard work and focus and a rage of a sort. Labor in the mind punctures and bruises emotion. I think that meaning is a human idea. Only a human one. Someone who thinks that can't be a messiah, right? No crucifixion for someone who advocates that—right? No.

A kind of disbelief afflicted some of the watchers such that I don't think anyone looked at anyone—much. I did now check the audience; no one looked excited or seemed talkative; words, even exclamations, even the use of one's breathing, the use of setting its tempo as a label for one's use of ordinary sight, for one thinking this is not an emergency, I don't have to be overly alert or whatever, all of that was unappealing and present. A few people did persist in absolute awe for a while, I would guess—maybe not: I have no real evidence from the world on this topic.

I think no one wanted to testify without letting some time pass first, really time for knowing better what had happened, for the newspapers and television to speak as The Seraph hadn't, for one's heart and one's life and one's dreams to express opinions and to allocate worth to this or that belief about things, to judge one's ambition to testify, and time to argue inside oneself first to see what one meant cloudily and as a start, and time to see what others said, to see what would work in the ages subsequent to the event in The Yard.

I did and did not *love* The Seraph, The Angel. Something so massive, so spectacular can take care of Itself. It told no one what to do, it was apparent from the clumsiness and abstractness and allegorical nature of the references to The Event that It advised no one and governed no language uttered in Its behalf. It had said nothing and It had vanished, and perhaps that meant It was best if one just let It go, that was what It had advised.

In the end, what was startling was that no one testified at the time. Or rather, it was all journalism and shock at first. And then came lyric attempts, and much cross-referencing back and forth.

Only after many years were there convincing but frail and as if whispered attempts at honesty, of which this is one.